Fetish

Dominant & Ta'iah

By

Nadine Frye

Copyrights

Acknowledgments

All praise and thanks are due to the Lord of the worlds. Without His light, I am nothing. I want to thank you all for your continued support on this journey. Writing this book was like giving birth. I tried to think of a way to bring light to some issues while also bringing something different and exciting.

This series that you are about to partake in will be stemming from a conversation about all the issues African American men face in their journey. Issues that, due to society and personal ignorance, get swept under the rug. Things, because of pride and the stigma placed on our men, that they are not supposed to cry or have feelings when things affect their hearts or change their perception. I wanted to write stories to battle that stigma and let our men know that you can share your pain, and it's okay to accept that you were a victim. It's okay to want to be loved. I stand with you. I love every one of you. This book is for

you.

-Nadine Frye

Prologue

I sat in the dark, counting down the minutes. Every Thursday night, it was the same routine. I'd tried to count sheep to no avail. Sleep still eluded my efforts. If only I could be asleep, maybe this would not happen to me. That was not true; Hatred's nature was just that.

Take.

Control.

Bend.

I wasn't expecting to be on the receiving end of another's unwanted desires, but every Thursday, since I'd arrived, had been full of darkness, filth, and spirit breaking. How many more Thursdays? I didn't know. All I knew was that Thursdays had become a repudiated time, and one I no longer looked to see them come.

I heard the voices upstairs, and it registered that Hatred's weekly activities were winding down. My heart began palpitating because, in mere minutes, my night would go from peaceful to chaotic. There was no preparation my young mind could conjure for the depravity that would come to corrupt me. All I could do was lie there, trying to force sleep to overcome me and hope I'd never wake again.

The front door closing echoed throughout the house, and the voices were now quiet. In the darkness of my environment, my breathing sped up rapidly, and my heart hammered in my ears. The lights were turning off, and it reverberated in the stillness of the night right before I heard the first footsteps.

Tonight, the footsteps were echoing, and the implications had my soul squeezed in fear. I squeezed my eyes tightly, praying to disappear before doom befell me. The whole time I wished with all my might, the object of my hate would fall and break their neck on their sick, depraved descent. As always, my prayers went unanswered, and reality gripped my heart.

The door opened, and the echoing footsteps were descending ever slowly, instilling fear with every thump on the staircase. A tear slipped down my cheek, but I hurriedly dried it because inside of these occasions, tears held no value. They didn't save you or appeal to humanity, and they only made matters worse.

I heard the exact moment Hatred reached the last step. Tonight, there would be no escape, so I adjusted my mind to become who I needed to be to get through Hatred's sick games. Emotionally, I'd learned to bury my feelings deep inside of my torn soul. They had no place there in a room where only the strong could survive. Hatred walked to the edge of my bed and gave its first command.

"Boy, up!"

Automatically, I got up out of bed and fell to my knees with my head bowed and eyes downcast.

"Ma'am," I responded docilely.

"Ooooh, he's trained well, I see."

The voice was new, and that gave me a sense of trepidation. Hatred never exposed its sickness to others. The new variable let me know that the game had changed, and I had but a moment to adapt.

"Of course, he is. Would you expect anything different from me?" Hatred asked its companion.

"No, I am impressed so far. Now, continue."

"Boy, stand." I stood while being sure to keep my eyes down and head bowed subserviently.

"You have trained well under my tutelage, and now it is time for you to show that my tireless efforts were not in vain. What is your purpose in life?"

"To serve your needs in any capacity, you need them served, ma'am." I responded with the asseveration Hatred instilled in me.

"Good boy. Is there anything that you will deny me?"

"Nothing will I ever deny you, and I'm yours to use as you will," I choked out but with enough conviction to convince my audience.

"Very well, boy. To the bench," she said dismissively. I hesitated and could hear her breathing change, which signaled Hatred noticed my apprehension.

"Boy, do we have a problem?"

Hatred's voice sounded laced with steel, and it made me move faster before things could escalate negatively. Once I reached the bench, I'd begun to undress before laying down with my arms and legs extended. My heart was racing in fear, but my need to survive made me complacent.

"Good boy."

Hatred moved around, getting her tools for this session. I waited with consternation to see what she had on her sick mind to do to me. Next, I felt the restraints as Hatred closed them around my wrist and repeated the *action with my ankles. When Hatred walked back to the top*

of the bench, my breathing became erratic.

"Boy, eyes up!"

I obeyed, and she was holding a wooden box. That

was a new toy, and undoubtedly one that would add depth

to the sadistic satisfaction she received from breaking me.

My eyes were laser-focused on the box as I awaited further

instructions.

"Boy, when I first saw you, those lips just drew me

in. I knew they would induce many nights of pleasure. Boy,

head up."

I lifted my neck at her command, and she placed the

box over my head and laid it back down. There was a circle

in the top that fitted over my nose and mouth but covered

my eyes.

"He looks so fucking hot, laying there. Get on with

the show. I'm going to enjoy this," I heard Hatred's visitor say with excitement, and it almost made me wretch in my mouth.

I heard a heavy shuffling of feet and clothes hitting the floor. Hatred was moving around, and then I felt the heat right above my face and the strong scent of French vanilla. The sweltering was getting closer, and then I felt lips touch mine, and they were warm and leaking stickiness as massive cheeks rested on my chest. The heaviness almost knocked the wind out of me, but I could still breathe. I hated the smell of Hatred on a Thursday night.

"Boy, tongue out and eat."

I wanted to throw up, but I'd learned the hard way to keep my stomach contents to myself. So, I extended my tongue and licked Hatred from top to bottom as she taught me. I gripped her clit between my lips and sucked and swirled in slow circles just as Hatred liked. Hatred started to pant heavily and gyrate her hips in excitement.

"Oh, yessss, you little bitch. Eat that fat pussy. Oh, just like that. Yesss, put your tongue in my hole. Yup, swirl just like that, you nasty lil' fuck."

Hatred always degraded me and still got enthusiastic like a true sadist. Hatred darted forward, and I felt its anus on my lips, and I didn't say anything, I ate whatever she put before me.

"Look, your boy is hard."

Why did Hatred's wretched companion have to say that? I had not mastered control of my body, and my involuntary reaction to the act was sure to set her off. Hatred went deathly still above me, and I felt the heat leave my face. Then I felt her breath hit my lower face as she whispered harshly.

"Boy, you little bitch, is this about your pleasure or mine?" I did not hesitate to respond

"Your pleasure, ma'am. I have no pleasure except what you give me, and only when I'm deserving."

"Then why is your big, black cock hard if I have not commanded it?"

I did not respond to her rhetorical question because no answer would suffice. My body's natural reaction to the stimulus was a blatant disrespect in Hatred's world.

Hatred moved down the bench and then reached over and grabbed my balls before twisting them. I swallowed the scream that tried to claw its way out of my throat. There was no choice but to take the punishment for violating her rules. Hatred snatched my penis and held it in a vice grip.

"What do we do with this thing now that it's here?" Hatred questioned its companion.

"Well, that pretty stick should be emptied."

I heard more movement then I felt a weight on my thighs. It wasn't Hatred, because Hatred was dense and stout. The legs on mine were lithe with a posterior that had influence but not overwhelmingly so. A delicate hand wrapped around my manhood before the thighs lifted off of mine. When they came back down, my strength was met by clinching walls that felt like fluffy biscuits drizzled with hot butter. My dick began thumping as she adjusted herself to accommodate my size.

"Boy, she is going to ride you, and rumor has it that she gets super wet, and you better not come before I make you. You got that?"

"Yes, ma'am."

Her friend lifted, and her walls clung to me on each upward stroke. It was almost too much, but Hatred's threat trampled my desire to cum. Hatred's companion was bouncing and getting wetter by the minute.

"Ooooh, this little young dick is so big and so good... Yes, stay hard just like that. Yesss, I'm about to cum all over this little dick."

Hatred's companion started cumming, but unlike Hatred, she was a squirter, and her cum reached all over my stomach and chest. She stopped cumming and got back

on my dick and started all over again. Bounce, bounce,

bounce, and spray at least four more times. I was getting so

close, but I modulated my breathing and hung on.

At some point, Hatred's mouth landed on my balls,

and her hands got frisky. I knew what was coming, and it

was the utmost humiliation, and Hatred would have it no

other way. Hatred's finger breached the rim of my

forbidden tunnel. I flinched as its fingers sought the nerves

on my prostrate.

"Boy, you like that, huh, you little bitch. You like to

feel my fingers inside of you, fucking you, huh. I knew you

were a sweet little bitch. You feel him getting harder, don't

you? Now cum you little shit."

I couldn't hold on if I wanted to, and like a rocket, I

blasted off, which sent Hatred's friend into a frenzy, and

she began cumming everywhere. I felt the tears slip out my

eyes at the sick shit that was surrounding me. Hatred

always played on my masculinity to keep me pliant and doing her bidding. I hated the bitch and all that it stood for.

Hatred's companion withdrew from my innocence. The rustling of clothes and shoes disrupted the silence before each of my limbs was released, but I stayed motionless until I eventually heard laughter and footsteps leaving the crime scene. At the same time, I laid there resolutely, trying to piece together my shattered pride. I had many thoughts of the innocence that I lost in the last two years and I was counting down the days until I could rid myself of the disease that was Hatred.

I got up and went to the shower and washed off the evidence of a grown woman's sickness. I hated myself every time and couldn't wait for the day when I could take control of my life. A day when I could forget, and I could live and be myself, and no one would be the wiser.

Chapter 1: Dominant

The energy spent opening up our new offices in Philadelphia had become a tedious task. It made me feel the urge to unwind. As half-owner of a major production company, this move was inevitable. It was bittersweet being back in my hometown, but I had a vision. A vision that I couldn't wait to bring to life.

It amazed me to own a building in Center City finally because it was something I'd only dreamed of having. My twin brother Justice and I used to come down here when we were young and pretend we owned it all. Those tall buildings were our playground and the leading role in our childhood fantasies. Now, we had moved up in the world and were ready to get our piece of the pie.

At thirty-five, this was a significant accomplishment in my life goals. We started by making a name for ourselves in Atlanta, and now we'd come full circle and opened another central office in our hometown. The journey here took plenty of hard work and dedication.

Ever since our spoken word tour, featuring my sister-in-law, came to an end, people had been trying to join our team in droves. We had interviewed all over the world, and now Justice and his wife were settled in Atlanta, enjoying parenthood. The outpour of talent we had received from the east coast made it necessary to open an office in a central location. There was no better place to live our dreams than where it all began.

I was putting things away in my desk when my cell phone began to ring. I already knew it was my twin, so I answered it quickly.

"Yo, Justice, what's up?" I asked him with enthusiasm.

"Nothing, bro. How are you?"

"I'm good. Just trying to finish setting up this office."

"Wow, you wasted no time, I see."

He knew how meticulous I was about everything. I needed to have order, and that included managing my time because there was none to waste.

"You know I like to get things done and out the way."

"Yeah, I know, bro…" Justice started hesitantly, and I cut him off because I had no time for guessing games.

"Justice, what's up with you? You got something on your mind, so out with it."

"Since you left, I've been wondering if you are okay back home in Philly. I know how you are concerning making changes."

"Why would I not be good with the changes?" I asked him, because that was a big assumption to make about me, someone who could adapt to anything.

"You always acted as if getting out of Philly was the only thing you ever wanted." I knew he was about to start psychoanalyzing me. "And although you never said anything happened to make you feel that way, as your twin, I always assumed it would come out when you were ready. Now I'm trying to figure out why the sudden change of heart?"

Justice was hitting home, but I was never going there with him or anyone else. I'd built my life and business by being an ultra-private person, and I could handle my shit. I didn't need my brother to engage me in a Dr. Phil session. I had my life under control, and whether he understood or not, my world kept moving. Justice would worry himself to death about me, so it's best to reassure him and get him away from this line of thinking.

"Bro, everything is good. Moving back here was the best decision financially, and you know I make moves that benefit our future. Twin, don't worry yourself about what it is or isn't I'm good over here."

"Everything ain't about money, and if you're not good, then you know you can tell me."

"Just, you are acting real chick flick-ish right now. You're making me feel all vulnerable and shit." I said this while laughing from my belly.

"Ha-ha-ha, you're always joking. What's wrong with me making sure that my little brother is good?"

"My G, you're all of three minutes older. You probably cheated getting out the womb. I remember being first and somebody pulling my leg, ole jealous ass, steal my thunder ass bul."

"Bye, Dominant, you play all damn day. I was first, and that's all I know, and you can't ever get a do-over."

I was glad we were on to other things. Some things I couldn't afford to indulge in nor acknowledge, and those were feelings. It took me many years to discipline myself this way. I hadn't felt anything in-depth since I left for college. Anything that required me to delve beyond surface interactions, I'd gone with all my childhood memories.

We talked for a while longer, where I inquired about his family and my new favorite nephew. We discussed our new artists and Pure's adjustment to the role of President of A&R. The call lasted twenty minutes before I'd made my excuses to get off the phone.

I had an important meeting to get to tonight. Tonight, was the night one of my aspirations would come into fruition. One that would cater to my true nature, and I couldn't wait to see my hard work come to life.

Chapter 2: Dominant

I was inside of the new condo I'd purchased in the Old City section of Philadelphia. Old City was usually reserved for those with old money, and although I was new money, I paid as I weighed. This area was central to a lot of eclectic tastes. If you had the money, you could indulge in just about anything, but with discretion.

What I'd planned to bring to the city may have been done before, but I intended to do it on a super-exclusive scale. My clientele had varying degrees of proclivities that might make society cringe. That's why I planned to create a safe space for them to indulge in their desires with no judgment.

Philadelphia served a dual purpose. Yes, our company was newly stationed here, but I'd been building a gentlemen's retreat for a little over a year. My club would cater to the elite of this city and provide every comfort their wealth could pay for with discretion.

I stood in my room, putting the finishing touches on my look. On my body laid a black suit, custom made to perfection, black shirt with a purple silk tie, and three-quarter-length shoe boots by Michael Grey Footwear. I added my cuff links and pulled my dreads into a man-bun and groomed my full beard. With a few swipes of a little Red Egyptian Musk, I was ready for the world.

When I reached the penthouse elevators, I took it down to the parking garage. On the way down, I got lost in the nervous excitement of revealing what I'd hoped to create. For the past year, I'd been working remotely with my real estate agent to secure this location.

After closing on this place, I had to hire an Architect, Interior Decorator, and Club Manager to work on my vision. All I did was give my insight and cut checks. It took a lot of Skyping and sneaking into the city to see my dream achieved. It had been a few months since I physically viewed the club, and I was hoping that this final walkthrough would be all that I'd imagined.

I jumped in my jet-black vintage mustang, and I was off to my destination. The club was built on the outskirts of the city in the Neshaminy section of Bensalem. It was practically in the mountains, and I wanted it that way to provide exclusive and secluded experience, as was needed to give my clientele security and freedom.

Forty minutes later, I pulled up to the black wrought iron gates of my new baby. I punched in my exclusive code, and the gates opened slowly. I rode up the gravel driveway toward the entrance of my building.

Outside, it was understated but elegant, and it was inviting. To the untrained eye, it looked to be a mansion that you would host parties in, but it was so much more. I parked my car in the driveway and stood there and took a gander at my surroundings.

The stone steps led to a high archway. I took the steps, and with each step closer, I'd become giddy with excitement. Once I was at the front door, I leaned in close so that I could have my retina scanned. When it came to the club, I'd spared no expense, and ensuring that my clients felt safe and their privacy was of the utmost importance.

The scanner beeped, and the door opened. When I walked inside, I was greeted by plush carpets in jet black. I walked down the stairs, and before my foot touched the last step on the landing, a little chocolate beauty greeted me. She donned a purple silk and lace nightie accompanied by garters and stockings in five-inch stilettos with her eyes downcast. In her hands, she held a tray with a single glass on its surface. She spoke to me in the softest of tones.

"Good evening, sir. Welcome to Your Inner Desires. May I be of assistance to you tonight?"

I grabbed the glass, and I saw that it is my drink of choice, which was Henny on the rocks with a splash of vanilla and exactly two cubes of ice. Grabbing the glass, I brought it to my lips and took a sip and swished the libation around in my mouth. It was perfect and just what I needed to unwind, and that earned her a smile from me.

"No, thank you, bunny. My drink was perfect. You may leave."

She never made eye contact, but I could see that she was gushing at having pleased me with a perfect drink. She bowed her head and retraced her steps out of the room. As she was leaving, I noticed her arm had a black band. That was too bad because it signified she was lightweight and not as durable as I liked them. So far, things were looking good.

I stepped into the foyer, and the chandelier was dim and interspersed with purple lights as I specified. There were also purple and black silk curtains hanging from the ceilings. It set the mood for creativity. I stepped into what was once the living room, which I turned into a cozy meeting place where all the fellas could have a drink and politic.

There were leather recliners and chaise lounges throughout this area that included a bar. Off to the side of the meeting area, there was a cigar room. Inside of this room, everything a man could ever need to wind down was in place. I stepped back out to begin touring the downstairs rooms.

Every room on this floor was for those who were into light playing. In the first room, there was a four-post bed with a sheer canopy done in black and silver with purple flowers. On the wall were feathers neatly stacked on shelves next to furry handcuffs and nylon ropes in various colors to match the color scheme. Next to the bed, there was an assortment of vibrators, bullets, and flavored lubrication. There was nothing extreme, and the room catered to light bondage play, prolonged releases, and having limits pushed with no pain. These rooms were for those subs who liked to be told what to do but had no real endurance or discipline for the heavy hitters. The *"Dom's"* who played here led with a soft hand and took pleasure from pleasure as long as they awarded that pleasure. Those patrons with black bands would enter those rooms and live out their fantasies.

After I completed the inspection of the last room on the first floor and saw the different variations of colors but the same themes, I was ready to move on. I went over to the stairs, and the staircase led up and then split into two sections on the middle landing. I decided to take the left staircase first.

This level was for our mid-level players who would wore purple wristbands. Dom's who played here would possess a firm hand interspersed with a gentle touch. Inside, the walls held feathers, leather handcuffs, ball gags, and leather floggers. To the side of the bed, there was a bondage bench equipped with leg and wrist restraints as well as a nightstand filled with nipple clamps, vibrating wands, candles, and assortments of gels and oils.

I left out and checked the other four rooms on the second level, and all of them met my standard vision and looked good. I exited the wings on the second level and ascended the stairs to head up to the third level.

I felt myself getting excited because this floor was for our gold-band bearers. For those of us who were immersed in this life and committed to the roles we played here. This wing was a testament to those men who needed control and were confident in the security and leadership they afforded a submissive.

This site was my baby and a direct reflection of who I became in this world. There were only three rooms on this floor. When I hit the top of the landing, I went to the room at the end of the hall. It was a room that would be my very own play area and sanctuary. I used my key card and walked in, and automatically, I was blown away.

My room had a color scheme of white, black, and silver. The ceilings were high and gave one a stately feel. There, suspended from a platform, in the middle of the room, was a large bondage bed. The bed was dark oak with four pillars in which both the lower and upper sections had attachments for my sub. To the left of the bed, there was a glass case built into the wall. In the case, there were whips in various sizes, from a Cat of Nine Tails to my personal favorite, the Leather Tigress.

Next, neatly stacked were my caning tools from polished oak to steel. Besides that, there were various gags and harnesses to posture collars, but the most beautiful piece in this whole display was a The Paddle, so I reached inside and picked it up, and the weight felt benevolent.

The Paddle was made of cherrywood and reinforced inside with steel. The handle was made from black Italian leather and made specifically for one with a firm grip. I turned it over and saw my name ingrained in the wood. My dick instantly hardened in my slacks. It was nothing like

seeing your name across a bitch's ass that gave a real sign

of ownership, and no feeling was more excellent.

I placed the paddle back in the case and finished

surveying the room. There was a bondage chair in the right

corner of the room with a pillory on the left side of the

room. There was a spanking horse equipped with a

retractable spreader bar. Next to the bed, there was a table

with steel and leather handcuffs, metal nipple clamps, silver

Ben Wa balls, anal beads, and blindfolds.

I walked back around to the front of the bed and

took a seat in the leather throne chair I had built there and

sat back and took it all in.

This room's design was heavenly and perfect for me

to indulge in my pleasure with a willing participant. I'd had

many subs under my tutelage, but none who could please

every facet of me. I needed someone who understood that I

craved control as much as they wanted leadership. Most of

the subs I'd found were kind and obedient, but they all eventually fell in love. Love was an emotion I didn't do personally. I needed my sub to understand that security, safety, guidance, and pleasure were all I had to give. If my next sub could adhere to my terms, then I would bring her into a world she'd never known could exist.

I took out my phone and dialed my club manager. He picked up on the second ring.

"Mr. Holloway, I take it the walkthrough was a success."

"Indeed, Jeremy, you have exceeded my expectations."

"Thank you, sir."

"So, we can go ahead with the schedule. How has the search for the girls gone for our exclusive members?"

That was another draw to the club. Each person who rented a room for a year on the purple and gold level would get the VIP treatment. We went through an extensive process to match each Dom with an individual who would meet every one of their needs. I liked to promote exclusivity because that was the only way trust was built in these types of relationships.

"Everyone is matched, including you."

That drew my attention because I could be insufferable and demanding, and it required a lot for a woman to grow underneath my leadership, but it was a necessity. Whoever this was had to be amazing and a veteran on the scene.

"Very well. Three weeks from today, we open, and then we shall truly see if you have done well," I said to Jeremy and ended the call

In three weeks, a dream would come true, and I would officially be who I'd always wanted to be.

Chapter 3: Ta'iah

I stood in front of my store, *Purrrfect Kitty*, preparing to open. My store was located in the South Philly section of the city on Columbus Blvd. When I walked inside, I disabled the alarm and went through to the back to drop off my things. Once everything was put away in my office, I walked back toward the front and started flicking the lights on as I made my way.

As part owner of a specialty sex toy shop, I knew that people tended to judge me. People thought that a thirty-year-old mixed Asian and African American must be into some "Taboo" things. Just because I happened to sell these items didn't mean I indulged in them. Who am I kidding? I had intimate knowledge of every piece of equipment that we sold in our shop.

My best friend and I knew that opening this store was unconventional. Especially if you measured everything by society's standard. Society said our store went against what two black women should do to earn income because sex was a subject for closeted conversation. I could care less what anyone thought because sex was liberating, and our products equaled freedom.

Sexuality and sensuality are things not often talked about because women were only supposed to be the receptacle for a man's release. Women were scared to enjoy the act, let alone have an opinion about the activities that took place inside of the bedroom.

Some women have never experienced orgasms because they don't know their bodies and are afraid to push the boundaries. Women, when it comes to sex or life in general, women loved being dominated. Just like we expect men to lead in life, we need a man to help us become our best sexually.

Most feminists would take offense to that thought, but it made it no less accurate. I loved nothing more than a man who stood in his royalty and could lead me in every facet of my life. It was like nirvana on earth and one of the reasons we opened this particular shop, and that was to help couples push their limits and receive equally beneficial pleasure.

The door chimed, alerting that someone entered the shop. When I looked up, a smile spread across my face. My business partner and best friend Anita had just walked in the door. If there was anyone who understood my thought process, it was her. Anita and I met through unusual circumstances, but our bond solidified over our love for our roles and the lifestyle choices we had committed ourselves. Kindred spirits we were, as well as sisters in this life.

"Hey, Best-Best, how art thou this morning?" I said to Anita while getting up to hug her.

"I'm good, Poodah. I'm just extra swamped this morning."

"Oh no, what happened?"

Anita handled all our online sales and orders. She also did consultations with clubs and different companies. Our product was in high demand because of its quality and originality. If you could think about it, we could custom make it.

"I have been on the phone for the last hour dealing with customer complaints and refunds. I don't think people read the descriptions when they buy the items," Anita said on an exasperated sigh.

"Probably not. Our products are known to cause excitement, so maybe they were too eager to try them out."

"I get that, but if you're bigger than the weight capacity, or you are unsure about how to use the equipment, and you try it anyway, that is not our fault. Now, you are stuck hanging from your feet instead of your hands. It is now what they call a fucking personal problem."

Anita had me laughing so hard because she talked so country, and the descriptions were too much. What Anita described had been known to happen with couples who thought that they knew how to use the equipment. We had a customer last week whose wife had her thighs stuck in a pillory. After calming the husband down, I had to explain to the consumer that the equipment wasn't used to bone your wife, but used for bondage and humiliation, and his reaction was priceless.

"Oh my God, girl, I know you gave them very detailed descriptions of its uses."

Anita liked to shock the clients with no experience for being idiotic enough not to ask questions before purchasing our items.

"You know I did. But that wasn't the biggest thing that happened this morning."

"Really, what could top that?"

"You know that new club that's opening?"

My heart rate sped up, and I knew my golden-brown cheeks were flushed red. I knew precisely what club Anita referenced.

"By your reaction, I know you know just which one. The club's manager called, and they need a special order of paddles and to change the crops they originally ordered to all leather. Guess what? We have until the close of business to get the order done. Someone will be coming to pick it up tonight."

That didn't leave us much time, but we were known to pull rabbits out our behinds on occasion.

"That is not an issue. I will go to the stock room and pull out all the paddles we have available. We just received a shipment on five different types of crops, all in leather. Now, it's just about the person coming in and choosing."

"Chile, you are a lifesaver. You know we don't want to make a bad impression since we will be joining their scene."

She never lied. You see, we were what you would call submissive or "subs" for short. Anita and I met as subs for the same dominant or "dom" for short, and he didn't have excellent leadership skills. That was important in these types of relationships. If a sub doubted your ability, she couldn't be led. A dom had to rule with conviction and provide her the safety and security she desired in their relationship dynamic.

We heard through the grapevine that a club was looking for subs for its exclusive clients. We both were required to fill out a questionnaire about our hard limits and soft limits. We had to go through a drug and disease screening as well as FBI fingerprinting and background checks. We both were fortunate enough to be matched with a dom, but we had no clue who. I was pretty excited about my match because from what information we were able to receive about their likes and dislikes, he seemed like the alpha I always envisioned.

"Right, I am going to begin pulling stuff down, and then you can help me get the show area together in between operating the counter."

"Uggghh, I knew I drew the short end of the stick."

Anita hated working at the front counter. She was a bit shy and awkward around anyone except me.

"Come on, Nita, somebody has to handle the customers. It won't be so bad," I said on a chuckle while heading to the back. Anita was muttering some choice expletives, which only made me laugh from my belly.

Once in the back, I began pulling down boxes. Time to think outside the box and get this task done.

Chapter 4: Dominant

Today was not my day. There was no level to describe just how pissed I was. It started with a meeting in which I had to fire the whole talent acquisition team for their incompetence in keeping in line with our company's goals and reaching their quotas. Then, I had to deal with an accounting issue at our Atlanta office that had me feeling like I was speaking alien. People and their ability not to use the brain they had indeed made my ass itch.

It was getting close to the time I needed to unwind. The feeling was just beneath my skin, and I'd begun to feel out of control. These feelings were unhealthy for me. I hated to feel like I was becoming unhinged. Like I was just a participator and not in control of my world.

I loosened my tie and laid back in my office chair and closed my eyes. It was getting harder not to lose my shit. While I was trying to gather myself, I heard my cell phone ring. I looked down at the offending device and saw that it was my club manager, and I begrudgingly answered the call.

"Speak." I knew it was rude, but I was in no mood for niceties.

"Mr. Holloway, I was able to get ahold of the specialty shop we used to design the rooms."

Okay, this is good news, and I was happy after the last walkthrough but noticed that the paddles and crops on the Purple floor needed to be changed. I liked things to be in order and to be fluent. I wanted nothing but excellence for my members.

"Okay, good. Were we able to secure the necessary items?"

"Yes, of course, sir. The owners have agreed to you picking up the items. She also called me back to let me know that they will be setting up the items so that you may choose what you need personally from what they provide."

Jeremy had indeed delivered good news. I ran across this shop online, and I was thoroughly impressed with their item selections. The craftsmanship, as well as the original takes on some essential equipment, led me to believe that whoever owned the store had express knowledge of the items. It was why I chose to use them, because it would lend to the authenticity of my scene.

"Very well, tell them I should be arriving around 8 pm."

"Okay, Mr. Holloway will do. I'll talk to you soon."

When Jeremy hung up, I blew out a relieved breath. I feel my control slipping back into place. Now I had to get through the rest of my impossible day.

***

It was around 7:45 p.m. before I could leave my office. I knew that I only had fifteen minutes to get to the store, but the world waited for me. So, I was not overly concerned about the owner's feelings.

I felt wound up tighter than a spring. What I needed to be doing instead of going to pick out toys, was a sub who could swallow me whole and take my stress away. That would be love right now.

My phone started ringing, and I saw that it was my brother. I was in no mood to answer, so I ignored him. It started ringing again, and it was blowing me because Justice couldn't be that fucking simple. What part of *I don't want to speak* was not indicated by my refusal to answer? It started ringing, and for the love of God, I was too pissed not to answer.

"Yo, bul, what's up with you?" I answered with sarcasm dripping in my tone.

"Do you care to tell me why the fuck you fired the whole *Talent Acquisition Team!*"

Oh, he called me big mad. I had to pull the phone away from my ear with how loud he barked at me. It had me looking for the person he would dare talk to in that fashion.

"First of all, lower them motherfucking capitals in your tone. Don't call my jack with the goofy shits 'cause you know I'm with them. Now, if you want to have a dignified conversation, address me like the king I am, or we can get right into this ghetto shit with no brakes."

Justice had to have taken leave of his entire mind. Talking to me like I was a damn child.

"Ok, my G, you want to be all in your feelings. You want to explain to me how you could decide for *our* company without consulting me?"

"First of all, I answer to no one. Secondly, the whole team was defective. The team was missing appointments, not responding to new talent queries, and they damn sure ain't been scouting shit. Lastly, I'm a boss, and firing and hiring is what I do. I won't have a bunch of lazy, incompetent num-nuts working under me. I am perfection, and I expect perfection. That's it, point, blank, period."

Justice made me grab my nuts and let him know what time it was. You don't reach this level in the game to end up back on the bottom. I heard him give a long-suffering sigh.

"Look, D, I get all that, but we are partners. All major decisions should be discussed just in case I can offer you support or a different alternative. I, of all people, know how you move. So, if they had to go, then they had to go, but don't forget to put me up on the game plan."

I could only laugh because he was acting so soft. This mushy conversation my brother wanted to have became super uncomfortable, so I started busting jokes to break up the emotions.

"Dude, I'm not your wife. I'm sorry that I didn't validate your feelings and all that good shit, but it is not that deep. I had it all handled, and there will be a new team in the office by the morning."

"Okay, that's fine with me. I just wanted to make sure everything was cool and we were still on schedule."

I was pulling up to the store, so it was time to cut our conversation short. I parked as I wrapped this conversation up. I had shit to do, and all this bonding was making me itch.

"You sure you good? Next, you're going to be asking me to hold your dick and cuddle you."

"Fuck you."

"Alright, then. I'm a call you tomorrow. I'm moving around, so I'm a get with you then," I told Justice.

"And, bro, I love you and will talk to you then."

"Olive oil juice too," I said while cracking up and hanging up the phone.

Marriage and kids were making Justice soft as cotton balls. That was why I was glad to be single and void from those frivolous emotions.

I was outside of the store, and its décor was cute. The sign had the store's name in white with the silhouette of a voluptuous woman bent over in stilettos with her hands in furry cuffs and a kitten tail out her rear end. That was one exciting logo, and it was inviting me inside.

The windows were tinted—no doubt to keep prying eyes out. I understood the need for privacy, as well as unwarranted judgments. I didn't know how some people were still so conservative when regular TV had more sex on it than was ever deemed appropriate. That didn't matter much, because people loved being judgmental, especially outside of their social norms.

I'd exited the car and made my way to the front doors. Automatically, I became who I was when I got into any business meeting. I knew how to draw a crowd and work a room. Whoever the owners were might as well be prepared to be my bitch. I took no prisoners when it came to business. I hoped they brought their A-game, because I was not easy to please.

Once at the front doors, I rang the bell and awaited a response. I stood a little taller and put my game face on. I didn't exactly wear a mean mug, but my look expressed that I didn't come to play games.

The door opened, and the most exquisite specimen stood before me. She stood five feet nothing, with clear caramel brown skin. I perused her from head to toe, taking in her wavy hair that flows around her face, chest, and past her shoulders. It was healthy and shining and a testament to proper hair care. She had on a t-shirt with her company's logo stretched across a perfectly perky set of C-cup breasts. Her shirt was tucked into her ripped skinny jeans, and I could see that her tummy was flat, and her waist was narrow. Lawd, she had hips, ass, and thighs for days. Her look was completed in a pair of black four-inch peep-toe wedge heels.

When I looked back up, I saw that the lovely lady was flushed. Then she stepped back, and I took that as an invitation inside. I moved forward, and she was not quite meeting my eyes. So, I spoke to grab her attention.

"Good evening. I have an appointment," I said commandingly, and I heard her inhale sharply, and her shoulders relaxed. When I saw her lashes touch her cheeks and her hands clasped in front of her, my antennas perked up. When she spoke, I was floored. Ever so softly, she said.

"Welcome to *Purrrfect Kitty*. I'm Ta'iah, and I am here to address your needs."

I felt my heart stutter and my dick stiffen. My face revealed nothing. Address my needs, she shall, and I hoped she was ready.

Chapter 5: Ta'iah

When I opened the door to my store, I was not expecting to feel this way. He devoured me with his eyes, and I shyly did the same.

He stood there four or five inches over six feet. Skin reminiscent of milk chocolate with a head full of dreads that were neatly pulled up and added to his aura of authority. He had a full beard and mustache that looked soft and fluffy. His lips were full and every woman's fantasy when she envisioned a grown man. He stood militant in a suit that was custom made and attested to him being one who possessed wealth and prestige. I could tell he was slightly bow-legged, and that made for a sexy walk.

His walk was not the most wonderful about the man, as his physique was nothing less than kingly. It was his presence, because I felt rather than saw that he was all man. His swag spoke of someone who asked for nothing but demanded everything. Dominant was a man that would have you looking for him in broad daylight with a flashlight and detailed directions. It was almost too much to bask in him, and I felt my cheeks heat up. He was all that, and every bone in my body was begging for me to submit.

I took a step back as he stepped inside. He filled my store up with his aura. His dominance was seeping into my pores, and I felt my pussy clench involuntarily.

"Good evening. I have an appointment."

He said it with authority as if he expected nothing less than the world to bow at his whim. I couldn't help myself, because I responded to what his presence demanded of me. I was always comfortable on my knees and ready to serve.

"Welcome to *Purrrfect Kitty*. I'm Ta'iah, and I am here to address your needs."

I told him with my head bowed, body slacked, and eyes down. Submission was ingrained in my DNA, and he was pulling it out of me.

"Very well, Ta'iah. I'm Dominant, and I understand that you have set up a demonstration of my requested items. Is this correct?"

Dominant spoke with confidence and authority. His tone brokered no argument from me, and it made me want to go the extra mile to please him in my demonstration.

"Yes, sir, I've set up an array of items that I believe will meet your specifications."

"Good, shall we see what you have set up for me?"

I led him into our lounge and stood next to a recliner, indicating he should sit. He chose the seat opposite of my choice, and it made me draw in a face and sigh. I hoped the demonstration went much better. For some reason I didn't want to disappoint him.

***

Dominant

I could see that Ta'iah was bothered by me choosing a different seat. She was so subservient, and I could usually judge women who pretended to be apart from those that were just hardwired that way. She had intrigued me with her demeanor, and I wanted to play.

My choosing a different seat was strategic. It was a test to see if Ta'iah would speak up or work harder at her task due to my displeasure. It was me asserting to her that I was never into anything, and I was the leader.

"You may begin."

Although it was her turf, it was a new ruling ground for me. Some would call my demeanor arrogance, but I called it King mode. Her nerves were rattled, and I could tell by the resigning breath Ta'iah took before she began.

"We understand that you were looking for exclusive paddles and leather crops. I have chosen three of our top sellers to present to you. Which would you like to see first?"

"You can begin with the crops."

She moved to the crops that were displayed upon a small, raised, royal blue stand. I saw her ponder over which one to choose before she grabbed the one on the bottom row.

"This crop is…" Ta'iah tried to say, but I cut her off.

"Basic, that particular crop is used to show more than being effective at meting out punishment. Next, please."

The one Ta'iah had chosen held a basic design, and I knew from experience that it would not pack the power needed for proper punishing. That crop would barely leave a mark. She turned back around and placed the instrument back in its place. Ta'iah's eyebrows were knit in consternation, and this time she took a moment to make a decision. When she turned to me, she bore a look of confidence across her face, and she demurely held out her choice.

I was delighted to see that she chose the one I wanted. The crop drew my interest because the design was unique. She began to break down the design.

"This crop is fourteen inches and is composed of leather infused with nylon with a steel cap on its end, which gives the user a sturdy grip. There is also a leather strap for wrist support to ensure that the grip is true. If you pay attention to the end, you will see that the crop has a webbed design. This crop is fashioned after the cat-o-nine tails, but it is firmer to give a perfect snap back and sting."

That sounded perfect to what I'd envisioned, but I needed to be sure that it was all she described it to be.

"Bring it to me."

She didn't hesitate to follow my command, and once in front of me, she placed the crop in my hand. It felt lightweight and well balanced. I put the strap over my wrist and tested it in my grasp. I loved the detail embedded in the tip. It would leave a beautiful mark.

"Ta'iah, open your palm."

Ta'iah's small palm snapped open, and she extended her arm toward me. I secured the crop around my wrist before I reared back to strike. There was a resounding crack as the crop rent the air and landed on her palm. Ta'iah didn't even flinch, and that was sexy as fuck. She was durable, and that was so my type.

"Let me see."

She extended her hand closer to my face, and I gripped her wrist gently to survey my work. I saw that her hand bore an intricate woven pattern. It was red, and the mark showed no sign of fading, and I was pleased with the tool.

"Palm down. I will take five of those once the demonstration concludes. You may continue."

Slowly, she walked back to the display. She was once again engrossed in selecting the item to show. I hoped she got it right.

Ta'iah

He was impressive, and the need to please him was riding me hard, so I knew that the next item I showed had to be perfect. My hand still stung a little bit, but I was a big girl and could take even more than that. Which one to choose? I would showcase my personal favorite—this next piece I designed myself. If my guess was correct, then he would be thrilled. I was a bundle of nerves, but I was confident I got it right. With my choice in hand and certainty in my ability, I turned to Dominant.

"This paddle is an original design. It's made from oak with a polished finish. There are grooves in the handle to keep the handler's grip firm and consistent on a swing. As you can see, each side has holes that line the wood. The paddle is reinforced with steel rings interlaced with leather so that it creates a suction in the middle. Here you will see that it has been double-branded with the word *mine* so that it will leave a pretty stamp on any area it comes into contact with."

I presented the paddle as I'd described the details. My breath was held captive in my lungs, waiting for Dominant to acknowledge my efforts.

"Hmmm, bring it to me."

I made sure to keep my eyes down as I moved toward him. I was a ball of nerves, but I made sure to keep my muscles relaxed.

When I reached him, I handed the paddle over and stepped back. Dominant took my offering and began to inspect the tool and test my description studiously. He seemed very sure and knowledgeable in his handling of the paddle, and his look was one of satisfaction. I got a little tingly at the prospect of meeting his standard. He stood up with the paddle comfortably resting at his sides.

"Good girl. This tool is fascinating. The craftsmanship is remarkable and unique in its design, but I don't think…"

"Sir, that design is more than capable of meting out any punishment. It will ensure that a bottom is sore and properly branded for at least a few days."

I may have spoken out of turn, but I knew that it was perfect for his club. He didn't respond to my plea for a while, and the silence was killing me. He only stared at me assessing me from across the seat before he set the paddle down then stood and removed his suit jacket. Dominant picked up the paddle and calmly retook his seat. The atmosphere became intense, and I didn't know how to react or what to expect until he addressed me.

"I thank you for your opinion, but it was completely unwarranted. I will decide on this paddle's effectiveness. Ta'iah, come."

He beckoned me closer, and just as before, I made my way closer with haste. I stood there, awaiting his direction.

"Eyes up…"

I lifted my eyes, and my peepers bore into his, and I was not ready for his next words.

"Remove your pants and bend over."

***

Dominant

Ta'iah appeared to be struggling with herself, but it didn't last long before she began to follow my command. I watched as she took off her shoes, and then, she reached for the snap on her jeans. She pulled them down, and they clung on her hips a bit because she was stacked.

Once her pants reached her ankles, I was pleased to see that she was wearing a sexy pair of black lace boy shorts. She stood there with her hands clasped in front of her. I tapped her left thigh, and she turned to the right before I gave her further instructions.

"On your hands and knees."

Ta'iah readily complied, and once she was kneeling, she pressed her face flush to the floor and deeply arched her back. The sight of her lying prostrate was titillating and had me wishing that I could take her home and own her completely. For now, this would have to slake my lust until my club opened, and I acquired my latest conquest.

I stood up and walked around her like a predator stalking its prey. Using the paddle as if it was my hand, I caressed her buttocks, and her cheeks jiggled like a wave rippling the middle of a pool. I lifted the paddle, and with a sure grip, swung and connected with her ass with a resounding whack. Ta'iah didn't even flinch, make a sound, or lose position. Who was this girl? Ta'iah had my curiosity piqued.

When I looked down, her thighs and the bottom of her ass cheeks that peeked out the bottom of her underwear, bore circular marks. The sight of her reddened cheeks was delicious, so much so that I reared back and did it again. This time when I surveyed my handiwork, I'd noticed the inside of her thighs were glistening, and her black underwear was stained creamy white in the seat.

"Does this feel good, Ta'iah?" She didn't answer me fast enough, so I let the paddle come down once more.

"That was a question, Ta'iah."

"Yes, sir."

"Hmmm, the mark is nice but not consistent. Take your underwear down."

She proceeded to follow my instructions. Quickly, she pulled the boy shorts down and went back to her original position. Once she was again kneeling, I used the paddle to smack her ass in rapid succession four times. The jiggle of her ass almost made me seasick, and her pussy was leaking onto the floor.

Once the ripples stopped, I perused the markings and saw the word "Mine" could be seen distinctively. I reached down to palm Ta'iah's cheeks with admiration as her body vibrated with the need for release. That was how I liked them—on the verge of losing it, awaiting my permission to let go.

"Indeed, you have chosen wisely. Be sure to order nine of these paddles, and the same for the crops. I will expect shipment before Friday."

I grabbed my suit jacket and left Ta'iah panting and shivering in the store. It seemed rude, but I knew I couldn't keep her, so there was no need to take it further. My new sub would greet me Saturday, and although tonight's entertainment was a distraction, it was time to focus on what was coming my way. Ta'iah would be the perfect sub if I didn't already have an obligation. The way she responded to my commands with little coercion was

surprising, and I wished I could have taken her with me. I

was going to file her away in my memory in case my

pending arrangement didn't work out.

Chapter 6: Ta'iah

It had been two days since that fateful night in my store. I was so dumbfounded when he left me on my knees, a blubbering, writhing mess. It didn't surprise me because most dom's took what they wanted and gave little thought to the cravings of a sub. The few moments that Dominant and I shared had me hesitant about going into my new situation. It was like one minute my ideal dom was molding me, and then the next, he was gone never to return. I'd been craving him ever since and a little sad.

Being this submissive had its drawbacks because all I wanted was the moldings of one man. One man to lead, protect, and free me. I wanted to know with certainty that he would take my trust and create a safe and comfortable environment for me to thrive.

The night Dominant left the store, I had to sit there and gather myself. His presence was paramount, and it almost consumed me. I had never been so wet in my life, and the floor became stained with my prurience. The way that he spanked me showed me that he was comfortable with leadership and that had me wishing that he'd allowed me a moment to sit at his feet.

Every whack was like a sensual caress. It felt as if Dominant touched me as one caressed a lover. All of me was in tune, and it had been a long time since I'd had any discipline. My thoughts had dispersed, and I almost begged him to take me with him. I didn't care if he put me in his pocket. I just wanted to breathe his air, and that feeling scared my thinking straight.

The truth was, in three short days, I would meet the new owner of my pleasure, and it was a point that made my heart overcome with happiness. It'd been years since I'd indulged myself in the BDSM scene, but after the brief interlude with Dominant the other night, I was more than anxious to get right back to my way of life.

I stood up and went to the dresser and took out my contract between my mystery dom and me. His identity would not be revealed until our initial meeting. The contract read:

Dear Ms. Harden,

You were chosen to enter into a mutually beneficial relationship between Dominant and Submissive in which you are the latter. Upon agreement to the terms that will be stated below, you will become Slave to the Dominant that has been delegated to you using our complex matchmaking system.

HYGIENE/PERSONAL CARE:

A. You will be required to be clean-shaven everywhere besides the crown of your head and eyebrows

B. You are forbidden to wear weaves, wigs or any extensions

C.   You will go weekly to be waxed and groomed at a location of the Dominant's choosing

D.   Any drastic change you wish to make regarding your appearance must first be approved by your Dominant

TIME MANAGEMENT

A.   You must leave a detailed itinerary with your Dominant of your work week or any activities you have planned

B.   All events must be approved by your Dominant before amending your schedule

C.   If your Dominant requires your attention at any time day or night, you will be expected to be available even if it conflicts with your schedule

RULES/SAFETY

A. As per your profile, we know that the only hard limits you have are Mutilation and Bestiality

B. If at any time you wish to stop any activity, your safe word is "Mellow." At which time all events will end, and you will be free from any business in which you were previously involved

C. Your wardrobe and accessories will be carefully selected for you

D. You will be required to check in with your Dominant via text when you awake and before you sleep and every three hours between the two events

E. There will be a color-coded light system to alert you which activity you will participate in at your Dominant's discretion. The list goes:

Purple- Bondage

Blue-Humiliation

Orange-Oral Fixation

Green-Spanking

Yellow- Prolonged stimulation

White- Combination of any activities

F.   You will remain sexually exclusive with your Dominant, and it is subject but not limited to Kissing, Touching, Dating, Looking, etc. This is to ensure that both parties involved remain free from disease.

You will be required to adhere to all rules placed before you, or it will result in the termination of your contract. Please sign and initial this form along with the Non-Disclosure Agreement attached and bring them with you to your initial meeting.

After re-reading the contract, you could hear my heart buzzing at the thought of my new proprietor. The rules were laid out clear and cut, and I couldn't wait for the opportunity to display my avidity to submit. I'd only hoped he would give me the platform to become all that he deserved.

CHAPTER 7: Dominant

Saturday had finally arrived, and I was in the zone in preparation for the possibilities. All of the items had arrived at the club on time like I knew they would. More than once, since the demonstration at *Purrrfect Kitty*, my thoughts had been overrun with Ta'iah. She was perfection, and I'd pondered often about breaking my current arrangement and seeking her out. The fact that I had her cumming just from a few well-placed spanks had me hard for days.

I had to shake out of the folly of my thinking as the reality was Ta'iah was not mine. No amount of foolish desire or unslaked lust could make that a fact. My new toy would arrive tonight, and she would greet me with the willingness to be molded, and that had to be my focus. I'd committed to seeing this through, and I honored my commitments.

Tonight, I would test limits and see if my new subject was bred for this life or if she only thought she was. The idea that I would only run into another poser was one that gave me pause, but I refused to believe this search was void. Disappointment lingered in the air, and I couldn't stomach failure. With optimism in my heart, I set about getting in the proper mind frame to welcome a fresh perspective

I headed into the shower and let the water wash away all the angst I felt. I grabbed my sandalwood and tea tree body wash and scrubbed myself clean. The scents went a long way to alleviating some of my stress. After that refreshing cleanse, I felt renewed enough to embark on my new adventure.

Once done with my shower, I hopped out and wrapped my body in a towel. On my bed, I'd laid out a white linen two-piece ensemble to compliment my chocolate skin. I'd placed my clothes on and went over to the mirror to check my fresh. My dreads were twisted up into a man bun, giving me a regal look. When my sub met me, she would understand she was in the presence of royalty.

I then dabbed on some Egyptian Musk and then grabbed my Gucci loafers on the way out. On the ground floor, I got inside of my black Chrysler 300 and drove over to my new club. The whole drive, I was buzzing with nervous anticipation of meeting my new "Kitten."

This week had been stressful, and I couldn't wait to utilize my new Kitten to alleviate it all. I knew that tonight was supposed to be about introductions, a simple meet and greet if you will. I didn't do things by conventional means, so tonight would be the first of many tests to see if she had what it took to be "Mine."

I arrived at the gate and went through the ministrations of checking into the club. Once I was at the front door and scanned in, I saw a hubbub of activity. Ladies of varying complexions were walking around, making our esteemed guests feel welcomed by addressing their needs.

I walked down the steps and headed into the man cave, and some of the faces were familiar, while others were not. Each step inside of the man cave led me to introductions and conversations with my members. On my way through the crowd, I spotted my best friend and headed over to him. He was happy to see me as I was him.

"Dominant, my main-man, what's going on?" My best friend's greeting was enthusiastic as we embraced in a friendly manner.

"Sterling, it's always great to see my folks," I responded to him as I released him.

Sterling Carter was a six-foot-three, light-skinned pretty boy with his waves spinning and even had freckles that dotted his cheeks. Sterling was a tech genius by day and an author by night who wrote panty-dropping erotica that had the women in the world singing his praises and lusting the fantasy he provided. His gimmick was no one knew who he was, as he wrote under a pseudonym and avoided book events and interviews. The mystery helped him blow up the charts, and everyone wanted to know the suspense surrounding his alter ego, Wet Dream. Sterling was also a gold bander like myself, and tonight would be monumental.

"This is amazing. Watching your dream finally come together is ethereal." Sterling complimented me on my efforts at bringing the club together.

"Yeah, it is wonderous. I never thought this would be anything but a dream," I told him honestly. At one point in time, I'd wanted to give this up as just a silly notion.

"I never doubted that you would, and it is pure genius. Now I can't wait to see if your team got our selections right."

"I hope no one will be disappointed, myself included. The team that chose the girls took the job very seriously concerning the selection."

"I have faith in you, but I'm just anxious to meet mine."

"Me too, and I hope she is perfect. You know how these women say they about that life until it's time to show and prove."

"Yeah, men with our proclivities are hard to please, and you, sir, are insufferable."

Sterling wasn't lying. I was very meticulous about everything in my life, and even more so when it came to women.

"Sterling, get out of here. Let's bust it up about business real quick. The girls should be arriving shortly, and I intend to be busy."

We had a seat and discussed our next moves. The ladies should be here any minute, and I couldn't wait to enjoy my night.

CHAPTER 8: Ta'iah

Saturday had finally arrived, and I was a bundle of nerves. I sat there listening to "She Wit the Shits" by Tank and trying to catch a vibe. I'd already showered and was sitting at the vanity in a towel rubbing edible Mango Cocoa Butter into my skin.

As I rubbed, the sound of the doorbell ringing cut through the air. I got up and went downstairs to answer the call. When I looked through the peephole, I didn't see anyone. I opened the door and looked down, and there was a beautifully wrapped package with a bag sitting on top. When I started to inspect the boxes, I saw that they were harmless, so I took them inside.

Once in my bedroom, I set everything down on my bed. There was a note attached to the box addressed to "Kitten," and I began to get excited. I tore into the letter and started reading:

Kitten,

Inside of this bag, you will find everything you need to meet me tonight. Please place your hair in a high bun and make sure your scent is subtle. You will be picked up promptly at 7 pm, so be sure you are ready as tardiness is not tolerated. I intend to do more than admire you tonight, so come prepared for anything.

-Your New Owner

Folding the note neatly, I then brought it to my chest and fell back on the bed and started squealing like a schoolgirl. With childlike excitement running through my veins, I went through the items in the bags and the box. Inside of the box laid the sexiest piece of lingerie my eyes had ever seen. I took it out of the box, and I was impressed with the lingerie's design. It was a Valentina strapless one-piece corset, done in leather and lace with a mini tutu train with the words "Daddy's Kitten" etched into the fabric. There were garters attached, and in the bottom of the box, there was a pair of pretty silk fishnet stockings as well as a Venetian half face mask with lace and feathers, which would obscure my face. I loved it and the mystery it would afford me. Carefully, I put the items back in the box and grabbed the bag.

Inside was a sexy pair of Red Bottoms, and I couldn't wait to put them on my feet. They were five-inch strappy heels in a suede peep-toe fashion. What I liked about them was the crisscross leather design with an elegant ruffle in the back. I think I just came all over myself. Nothing got a woman going like a sexy pair of shoes.

After placing the items on my bed, I headed over to my vanity to prepare my makeup. I chose to go with a natural look. Just a light dusting of powder and a smoky eye to make my slanted eyes pop out. I decided to use a dark purple matte lip color to blend well with the dramatization of the outfit and to make my already plump lips inviting.

Once I was finished, I unwrapped my hair. Initially, I wanted to wear my hair out in big curls, so I put Flexi rods in, but Daddy wanted a bun. I began taking my rollers out, and once done, I ran my fingers through the curls to give them some fullness and bounce. I enjoyed them for a moment before grabbing a wire brush to begin pulling my hair into a high bun as per his request.

I raced back over to the bed and began to get dressed. With each item I placed on my body, I felt more confident and wholly owned. To know that my dom took the time out to pick these items just for me put me in a very generous mood. I couldn't wait to show him my gratitude.

I placed the shoes on my feet and buckled them as I stood in front of the mirror. My C-cups were sitting lovely, and my dragonfly tatts were playing peek-a-boo on top of my stockings. I placed the mask on my face, and I was in love with his tastes. I turned around and grabbed my clutch, putting my phone, cards, and keys inside.

With ten minutes to spare, I checked to make sure everything was off and locked down before I stepped outside at exactly 6:58 p.m. and secured my door. When I turned around, there was a LA Custom Coach Black Dodge Challenger SRT 8 pulling up to my curb. Ooh, that thing was a sexy sight. The driver walked to the bottom step of my townhouse, so I walked down to greet him. As soon as my foot hit the last level, he reached his hand out for mine, and I placed it in his and escorted me to the car. Before we reached the door, he went into his breast pocket and retrieved an envelope and handed it to me.

He opened the door, and I stepped inside, making sure to tuck my train. He closed the door and went around to get back into the driver seat. I looked inside, and there were six ladies, one whom I recognized even with her mask. I was so excited to see my best friend.

"Oh my god Anita, I thought I would only see you on the inside of the club."

I lamented while reaching over to hug her, and she was looking good in a red and black latex short jumpsuit with a pair of thigh-high boots. Her mask was red and black and covered the left side of her face. She looked fierce, and I loved it.

"Yessss best-best look at you, slayyyy, bitch," Anita told me while doing a little twerk in her seat.

"Thank you, best friend. Wow, this car is nice and cozy."

"Yes, and the amenities are nice. Did you read your note yet?"

"No, so everybody got notes?"

I asked the ladies in the car, and everyone nodded in the affirmative. So, I took the envelope and opened it before I pulled the note out and began to read.

Ms. Harden,

Tonight, you embark on a new journey. Your Dom has only been given preliminary info about you. He does not know your name or have any idea who you are, so it will be up to you to make an excellent first impression. You and the other ladies have all been provided a number. Yours is 4. When you enter the mansion you ladies should line up left to right according to your number, and this will be how you will identify who it is that will own you. Make tonight one to remember.

I put the note back inside and then looked to my best friend and just smiled.

"So, what is your number?" I asked Anita

"I'm number five, and you?"

"I'm number four, so you will be to my right, and which one of you ladies will be to my left?"

"That would be me, lucky number three."

The speaker's voice was husky and the true definition of a bedroom voice. I turned to her, and she was in a royal blue and black satin bustier tucked inside of high-waisted royal blue pants with strategic slits on the side tucked inside of a badass pair of five-inch black suede peep-toe ankle booties. She was chocolate and had her hair pulled up into a sleek, high bun. Her mask was Mardi Gras inspired with the feathers fanning out so beautifully like a peacock. I reached over and extended my hand.

"Hi, I'm Ta'iah, and you are beautiful."

"Thank you! I'm Zahra, and you're looking like a snack yourself."

Her response had me laughing out loud, and for the next thirty to forty minutes, we vibed out. There were many different personalities in the car, and the vibe was all sisterhood. Anita and I learned that Zahra owned an online lingerie shop, and we were wearing a few of her pieces. The intricacies in all of our outfits were super creative and a testament to the brilliance of her mind. Anita and I told her about our specialty toy shop and how a majority of the rooms in the mansion would have our items in them. We exchanged numbers and discussed a possible business venture in the future.

We pulled up to the wrought-iron gates of the mansion. I was taken aback by its opulence, and I stood in awe of its grandeur. We were all speechless as the driver exited the car to come around and open the door for us. We all exited the vehicle, and once we were all there, I turned to the ladies and said.

"Okay, ladies, it's showtime."

Chapter 9: Dominant

Sterling and I had been in a heated debate about the stock market when our other best friend Zuri Williams joined the party. Zuri was six feet tall with skin the color of peanut butter, that attested to his mixed heritage, with a curly top that was tapered into a mohawk on the sides. He was a business tycoon who specialized in acquisitions. Zuri had always been a go-getter, and whatever he set his mind out to do, he accomplished with little to no effort. He could rescue your company or take your throne and make you his worker. Zuri was an asset as a friend and a nightmare as an enemy. His ass was always late to the party, but with the girls almost arriving, I guess he was right on time.

"So, what's with the numbers that we were given at the front door?" Zuri asked.

"My manager said that's how we will realize which girl is ours. We're supposed to line up from right to left according to the numbers."

My manager had gone above and beyond as far as making this experience unique and mysterious. I might have to give him a raise.

"Well, what number did you get?" Zuri asked me.

"I got four, and you?"

"I got three, and what about you, Sterl?"

"I got five," Sterling replied.

"Man, that's wild. Three the hard way even while we play."

Zuri was forever the jokester, and he elicited laughs with no effort.

"You already know. What do you guys plan on doing as an introduction to your lady?" I posed the question to my main guys, trying to see where their heads were at in this game.

"Man, I want to see if she can take the pain. That is important to me, and we won't have anything to discuss if she can't weather the storm I'm going to bring to her," Zuri said, and I understood his need, because his story was a deep one.

"Well, I want to see if my girl can play in a fantasy setting. I plan to test her ability to adapt at the drop of a hat. And what about you, Dominant?" Sterling said and leave it to a creative to want to play dress-up on the first night.

"I haven't decided yet, but I want to see how well we mesh. I will take my Kitten through a few paces and rely on her cues to tell me where to lead her next," I replied.

"Well, fellas, it's time we made it out to the foyer and met these ladies," Sterling reminded us before leading the way to our meet up point.

So, the other men and we go to line up in the foyer according to our numbers we received. We formed an open-ended triangle shape with me at the center and Sterling at my left and Zuri on my right. I felt my anxiety skyrocket with the excitement of seeing my mystery lady in the outfit I chose for her. I had my best guys with me, and we looked ready for the world.

At 7:45, the door opened, and the ladies proceeded to come inside and chose to line, with no prompting, to mirror our formation, and that was amazing. My counterpart looked stunning in the purple and black ensemble I'd selected with her hair in a thick, high bun, and I couldn't wait to see it undone. The mask made her look elegant as she stood with her body fully relaxed and head slightly bowed awaiting instructions.

I raised my hand and beckoned her to come to me. My Kitten began to walk down the steps, and when she reached the last level, I pointed down. She automatically dropped to her knees with her hands folded in her lap, and her head fully bowed. I walked to her and began to stroke her hair, and she started to rub her face upon my thigh, relishing the attention I showered down on her. I stepped back and reached my hand down for her to grab, and then I helped her to my feet.

"Good girl. Daddy is impressed, now come," I said before turning to walk away.

I didn't even have to look back because I knew her obedience would be automatic. I'd proceeded up the stairs and used my key to unlock the gold section. We went down the hallway until we reached my door at the end of the hall. I walked inside and held the door open for her. My Kitten walked in with her head bowed and ambulated to the side of the door. Once the door was locked and secured, I moved in front of her and gazed at her subjectively.

Her eyes were alight with happiness behind the mask. My Kitten was bouncing from one foot to the other as her head moved around, taking in the sights of my domain. The lights were dim and highlighting the room and the splendor it displayed. I had something set up in another place, but it appeared she would like to stay here and play.

Very soon, she would be able to enjoy what the room

offered, but for now, we would get to my setup.

"Kitten follow me. We are going right through

here."

We then proceeded to the next room, where I had a

table set up. The table, by right, could seat at least eight,

and it was a massive oak design with intricate carvings of

various stages of intimacy between a man and woman. The

way the designs flowed into each other was what drew me

into purchasing it. I only had two high-back chairs at the

table. Mine sat at the head of the table, and it was very

pretentious and stately, and it was lined in velvet and fit for

a king. I had her chair placed on the right side of mine.

Our place settings were on the table minus the food.

I had a little buffet set up with chicken parmesan, roasted

Brussel sprouts, a rainbow veggie salad, and homestyle

biscuits. My favorite drink was on ice, ready to be

consumed. My stomach began to rumble at the delightful

scent, wreaking havoc on my senses. It was then that I realized how many meals I'd missed in anticipation of this day.

I took a seat in my chair and got comfortable, and she moved closer and stood to my right. Her hands were folded neatly in front of her, and her posture was predisposed, just awaiting my instructions. My body took notice of her subservience and the mannerisms she displayed, and I was pleased.

"Kitten, I'm hungry."

Instantly, she picked up my plate from the place setting and then moved to the buffet to prepare my dish. Her movements were swift and deliberate, and when done, she turned to me and placed my plate in front of me. My plate donned perfect portions, and none of the food was touching, which was a pet peeve of mine.

"What dressing would you like for your salad?" she asked me gently.

"Balsamic vinaigrette would suffice."

Hurriedly, she went to retrieve the dressing as well as my drink. Once she placed my glass next to my plate, she moved to remove the dressing. Then she returned and resumed standing next to my chair. I took a bite of my food and a sip of my drink, and I was pleased.

"Thank you. Everything is fine. Go and make your plate and join me."

She picked up her place setting and quickly made a plate and returned to join me. When she sat down, I noticed that she only piled her plate with chicken parmesan and the rainbow salad with Caesar dressing on top and a cup of water.

"Remove your mask and get comfortable. I intend to get to know you."

I craved to look in her eyes and enjoy her beauty while I got to know what she required of me to be effective as a leader. Her hesitation was noticeable after I'd given her the command to remove the mask. That was the first time tonight that I was met with resistance, no matter how slight. She raised her hands and slowly started to remove her mask with her head turned in the opposite direction. Once the mask was off, she sat it on the left of her plate. When she turned to face me, I saw the reason for her hesitancy, and it caused a sinister grin to spread across my face. Oh, I was going to enjoy myself thoroughly.

"Ta'iah has been a bad little kitten, I see."

Chapter 10: Ta'iah

My breathing had become erratic once the mask was off. When I walked in and saw the man of more than a few wet dreams, I knew that it was fate. Who knew that the owner of this club would be my match? I went into tonight with no expectations, and I honestly thought I would never see him again. Just thinking back on that night had me shivering in my seat. I'd started to feel very apologetic because, in reality, I was obligated to him the night he showed up to my store. However, I didn't know it was him, but I still felt like I cheated.

"Sir, I…" I began, but he interrupted me.

"Daddy," he stated firmly.

"Daddy, I would like to apologize. I assure you that I didn't know who you were nor whom I was obligated to on the night you arrived at my store. If I had, I would have acted more appropriately upon meeting you," I rushed and said.

"But you were obligated none the less, am I correct?"

"Yes." I whispered the affirmation

"I can't hear you, and address me appropriately. You did know you were obligated to someone?"

"Yes, Daddy, I did." I responded more confidently.

"Very well, there will be more than enough time to apologize and atone for your actions. Now, I would like to eat, enjoy your company, as well as get to know you. So, tell me about yourself," he said, switching subjects, but my mind was stuck on apologizing.

"What would you like to know?"

"Start generally, and then if I need to know more, I will ask."

"I'm twenty-eight years old and part-owner of *Purrrfect Kitty*. I come from a mixed cultural background. My mommy is Asian and Indian, and my father is African American. I'm an only child," I began.

"Did you enjoy being an only child?"

"I did. I was able to observe more, and it is cool not having to vie for the affection of your parents."

"I can see that. How long have you been a submissive? What made you interested in that role?"

"I can honestly say my home life made it natural. My mother never raised her voice to my father in anger or in general. She provided all of his needs without him ever asking. She took care of his home without complaint. Whatever my father faced outside the home did not continue once he crossed his threshold. She was truly his peace. My father is a manly man, an Alpha male if you will. He worked hard to provide a comfortable life for us. He was a fierce protector and treated my mother like a queen. He is a great leader, and their system worked. I don't know about their sexual proclivities, but their home was happy, and I was glad to see that."

"So, it's just as I originally thought. You were born to do this." The admiration in his tone made me feel right to my core. It let me know that we were off to a good start.

"I like to believe so because the example they set had me seeking that through my intimate relations."

"What is important to you in this dynamic between dominant and submissive."

"My ideal dominant would lead with a firm hand. Most times, doms drop the ball and can't offer thorough leadership. I'm extremely submissive, and a true dom presents himself throughout his aura. You can't expect a willing student if you have not the tools to lead them," I told him honestly.

"Has this been an issue before?"

"Yes, I can't be who I need to be if I don't have good leadership."

"Interesting. Do you have your contract?"

I reached for my clutch and handed him the signed contract. He took a moment to peruse the agreement before he then folded it and placed the contract in his pocket.

"Everything looks good. Now I'm more than confident that I can lead you where you need to go. All I ask for is loyalty. Loyalty is of the utmost importance to me. For me to be effective in my role, I need your complete trust and no questions. Anything I do for you or to you is for your benefit. Do you think you can do this?"

"Yes, I can."

"Very well, clean up this table and meet me in the next room when you are finished."

He walked out, leaving me to the task he had given me. I grabbed our plates and disposed of them in a bin that sat there for the purpose. With him in another room, I became nervous. I didn't know what to expect, and trepidation began to set in as I overthought the process.

Once I finished cleaning up, I took a few deep breaths and prepared myself to go into the next room.

When I walked into the room, I saw that it was white, which meant that he was going to use a combination of methods. Dominant stood there with his shirt off with a body perfectly sculpted accompanied with a deep V-print at the end of an eight pack. He held in his hand the same paddle he used in my shop. He stood beside a bondage bench, and I stood there with my eyes lowered, waiting for his instructions. The silence was deafening, and I didn't think I was prepared for what was to come.

"Am I to understand that you willingly engaged in sexual activities while you were indeed obligated to me?" he asked in a deathly calm voice

"I didn't know…" I started trying to explain myself, but he cut me off.

"Did you or did you not is the question. I didn't ask you what you knew. *Now answer me!*" His eyes were emotionless as he yelled in a voice that demanded an answer quickly.

"Yes, daddy."

"Get on the bench, face down, and put that arch in your back."

I proceeded to the bench and placed my knees upon it. Bending over, I set my cheek and breasts upon the bench, which caused my ass to rise higher and a deep bend to form where my top and bottom half met. My insides were on display with how deep I bent over. I felt Dominant sit the paddle on my ass, and it stayed in place as he moved away.

He began moving around me like a predator stalking his prey. His hands traversed my skin from my thigh down to my ankle. Then I felt the coolness of silver upon my skin as he handcuffed my ankle. Dominant repeated his ministrations with my left foot, and he locked me down. A shiver passed through me, and I felt vulnerable but ready to take what he had to give.

"Place your hands behind you."

I did as he said, and he cuffed my hands to my legs. That made me turn my chin and stare straight ahead. He pressed a button that raised the bench where my chin rested, causing discomfort. Although uncomfortable, I didn't mumble one word. Dominant came and stood in my line of vision, and I was face-to-face with his pelvis.

"When I enter into these agreements, I demand a certain type of loyalty even in absentia. I take exclusivity very seriously. What you did would have made me dismiss a submissive, but I do understand the draw I have, so if you can survive this punishment, all will be forgiven. Do you think you can handle daddy's punishment?"

"Yes, daddy," I responded and hoped my words rang true even though I held some uncertainty.

"Very well, being as though you didn't speak up the night we met, I have to see if your mouth is in working order."

Dominant took a step back and dropped his pants. He was wearing a pair of boxer briefs that barely concealed the monster hidden inside. The sight alone made my mouth water. Slowly he pulled down his briefs, and saliva was dripping out of my mouth in anticipation of the first taste. Dominant was blessed, and you rarely met a man who had length and girth, and he had the nerve to have both. He was clean-shaven, and that was such a turn on. He approached my face then used his fingers to caress my plump lips before lingering on the bottom lip and pulling it down.

"Open your mouth. Tonight, you are going to eat this dick while I pleasure you, and if you cum before I permit you, then you will leave here and never see me again. If you do as I say, then I will keep you, and I really would like to do that. Do you understand me?"

I nodded my head in affirmation, and clearly, that was not appropriate because I felt him bring the paddle down and smack my ass viciously.

"That was a question!"

"Yes, daddy, I understand."

"Open wide."

In compliance with his request, I opened wide as he began stroking himself from root to tip, making the veins more prominent. He then proceeded to feed me the dick inch by inch. I flattened my tongue and used my lips to cover my teeth. He set a steady pace of in and out, and my saliva made it wet and nasty for him. Dominant's tumescence hit the back of my throat, and I didn't blink an eye or gag once. Once he noticed that I had no gag reflexes, he lost his mind.

"Oh, shit, bitch, I'm about to knock the lining out of your throat."

After that declaration, he began to fuck my mouth relentlessly. He buried himself balls deep into my throat and held position. With his hand, he began massaging my throat to feel himself and then released himself to start again. As he was fucking my throat, I could feel the area where my legs were separate. With my legs spread apart, my middle dropped lower, and I could feel my pussy touching the table.

The table began to vibrate against my pussy at high speed, and it shocked me speechless. I almost lost the groove of having my face fucked. I looked up into his eyes, and I could see a smirk on his face.

"You thought it was going to be easy, huh, Kitten. You better hold on because I'm not nearly done."

Oh my God, my eyes rolled back as my legs began to tremble. With the added vibrations, I could feel my skin break out into a blush as the sweat sheened my skin. My thighs began quaking right before the waves stopped. My clit was throbbing like a heartbeat, and my juices poured down my legs.

Dominant started tugging my hair as he stroked my throat with fervor. He pinched my nose and held it closed, which caused me to lose oxygen and my body to wrack with euphoric spasms, but I wasn't cumming. I would do anything to win, and my will to stay had me holding my orgasm in, to the brink of pain. I felt him tremble slightly, but he relinquished nothing as he stood tall.

The table vibrated again, and I just knew that he intended to kill me. The speed went from high to low in rapid succession, and my nerve endings began to hurt from holding my orgasm inside. When he finally permitted me to let go, I knew I would be eviscerated.

"Oh, you're a perfect little bitch. That's right. Eat. This. Dick. Just like that."

I had to find a way to get him to end the torture, so I clamped my throat around his dick and hummed. My antics caught him off guard, and Dominant let off down my throat involuntarily. What surprised me was that he didn't get soft. My eyes widened in surprise, and he chuckled.

"You surprised daddy, but I'm a grown-ass man with stamina for days. You swallowed all of my seeds, and how did they taste?" he asked me while removing himself from my throat.

"Just like dessert," I answered a little breathlessly because the vibrations from the table were driving me insane. I was barely hanging on.

"Awwww, Kitten, would you like to cum? You don't look so good." He taunted me with a smirk on his face.

"Yesssss, please."

"I would like to let you cum, but I don't think you're sorry enough."

He slowed the speed down once again, and my clit was sore from the extended stimulation. My muscles were exhausted, and I'd become dizzy. Next, I felt something moist and warm flowing between my posterior.

The lubrication paved the way for the anal beads that he began to insert into me slowly. Dominant started a rhythm of increasing and decreasing the speed of the vibrations of the table while inserting and tugging out the anal beads. My mind felt ready to explode, and tears left my eyes as I tried to hang on to my orgasm. If I didn't, inevitably, I would lose the opportunity to be under his tutelage before I ever knew its greatness.

"Kitten, understand I don't like lies. Even ones told by omission, and your loyalty is everything to me, and I don't ever want to question it again. Are we understood?"

"Yes, daddy."

"Now you have until the count of five to make it rain everywhere."

He didn't even make it to two before I blasted off like a rocket. My body levitated off the table, and a tsunami erupted from my pussy. I had never come so hard in my life.

"Good girl. Now I will bathe you."

Gently, Dominant untied me and helped me from the table and led me to the bathroom. When I stepped inside, I was in awe of its exquisiteness. The bathroom was like an oasis for women. I noticed some of the same products I used at home, as well as any sponge or loofah you could imagine.

He set the shower and instructed me to get inside. When I saw him getting undressed as well, I became a bit confused, but I stood under the spray and awaited Dominant's command. He took a loofah and sensually washed me from head to toe. Then he started my hair, even conditioning and combing through my curls. I was overcome with emotions and began to cry. Dominant turned my face toward him and stared confused as the tears rained down my cheeks.

"Kitten, what's wrong? Are you not satisfied?"

"I am satisfied beyond measure. The way you care for me makes my soul happy. You're perfect, and I can only hope to be the same for you."

"It is my job to take care of you, and I will do that with the utmost care and attention. Now let's go home."

You could hear the delight in his voice when he spoke to me. Dominant cut the water off and then rung out my hair and helped me out of the shower. Then, he dried me off and placed a new dress and shoes on the bed for me to don. Once we dressed, Dominant took me through a back entrance that led us outside. After we got to his car, he strapped me in and went and got in on his side. No words needed to be exchanged as we drove off into the night. At that moment, I'd decided to trust him entirely as he led me to new territory.

Chapter 11: Dominant

Ta'iah was terrific, and she took her punishment like a big girl and even passed my self-control testing. Her passing my test gave me confidence that she was ready to enter into the next phase of our partnership. Had she not passed, I would've had the limo take her home and give her a nice little severance. Since she passed, she got to come home with me. I believed I had her pegged correctly and that her response to what I'd hoped to propose would be favorable.

We pulled into the underground parking for my condo. I parked my car, hopped out, and headed around to open her door. I reached in to help her out, and then we headed into the elevator and up onto the penthouse floor. Once we arrived and stepped inside, Ta'iah stopped. She stood in awe of my sanctuary and her eyes took everything in with delighted wonderment.

"Shoes off." She proceeded to take her shoes off, then without prompting, dropped to her knees to remove mine. Ta'iah sat on her haunches and awaited my next command. All I could think while watching her was that this was going to be a perfect arrangement.

"You can stand. Come on so I can show you where you will be staying for the duration of this arrangement."

I walked her through the condo, helping her get acquainted with her surroundings. Our tour led me to the room I'd had set up for her. I'd designed the room in purple and silvers, with a king-size sleigh bed with sheer drapes that hung over the top. I had an antique vanity placed here with an armoire and chair. The room was stately and set to make her feel like a queen. Although her whole purpose and desire in life would be to please me, I intended to take care of her in a manner that would make her submission effortless.

"I need to have you close to ensure that you are safe and cared for to my standard. I only require you to follow the rules that I will lay out for you over breakfast in the morning. Is there anything that you immediately need before I retire for the night?"

"No, daddy, everything is lovely and perfect. I can only hope to show my gratitude for the care you have given me."

I went over to her and gave her a little affection as a reward for her acquiescence. Her eagerness stroked my ego and kept me hard.

"You're already showing me. Just continue to allow me to lead you, and everything will be fine. Time for you to get ready for bed. Read the information I left on your vanity, and I will see you at 6 a.m. sharp. Goodnight, Kitten."

I kissed her forehead and left out of her room and headed into my bedroom. Nighttime was usually the time when sleep eluded me and had me running from my past. Bedtime was the playground for my demons to replay on a never-ending reel.

After grabbing a pair of pajama bottoms, I slipped my clothes off and prepared to get ready to war with myself. I slid underneath the covers and laid ruminating with my eyes focused on the ceiling. Every night, it was the same thing, so I settled in to await the usual torment. Instead, visions of Ta'iah began to play.

The way she obeyed without coaching was what my heart desired. Tonight, watching her control her senses strictly for my pleasure, was poetry in motion. Never had I had a woman this pliant nor this willing. It was as if she waited her whole life for my leadership. If I were healthy, then she would be the perfect life partner. I would never be able to give her that. But what I had to offer her would be worth the sacrifice of never having more. If I had it my way, she would be mine forever just the way we were. My leadership combined with her submission and our life would be magic.

Those thoughts were the last I had before sleep overtook me. For the first time in years, I slept like a baby.

Chapter 12: Ta'iah

Last night when I got into my room, Dominant had left a note that told me, as part of our agreement, it was a requirement for me to stay in his home. That explained the trouble he went through to make sure my accommodations were suitable. If I agreed to his terms, he would see me in the morning for the beginning of our daily routines. It was a no brainer, so I went to bed straight away to make our first morning memorable. After walking through the detailed steps he left me a million times, I fell asleep.

I'd awakened at 5 a.m. and prepared myself for what was to be my morning routine. I was kneeling beside the right side of Dominant's bed, dressed in a silk nightgown waiting for the alarm to ring. My hair was out and wild per his request. It was a little early for my presence, but my excitement had me up before the sun, and now I watched him sleep, and it was quite interesting. Dominant slept on his back with one hand in his pants and looked utterly ordinary. His chest was on display, and he was divine on the eyes. I was going to love waking him up in the mornings. I heard the alarm sound, and automatically he opened his eyes and peered right at me.

"Good morning, Kitten. Are you hungry?"

"Good morning, and yes, I'm starving."

"Come, let daddy feed you."

I placed my hands behind my back at the same time that he stood. He dropped his pants, and my mouth began to water. Putting his hands in my hair, he started feeding me dick. The deeper he went, the wetter my mouth became. I began to relax my throat muscles because I wanted to eat it all. He wasted no time fucking my face and taking advantage of my absent gag reflexes. Very soon, he was cumming, and then he pulled out of my mouth with a pop. I showed him all his seeds on my tongue and then swallowed them as if he fed me a five-star meal.

"Good girl. Let's get on with our day."

Dominant stepped out of his pants and went into the bathroom. I already had his bathwater set, and I picked up his pants to put them in the hamper before joining him in the bathroom to start his grooming. I washed him from head to toe, then I shampooed and conditioned his hair. I was rubbing his scalp to stimulate his roots thoroughly. Once I finished, I let his water out and then went to start his shower.

After watching him rinse himself entirely from head to toe, I grabbed two towels. One for his waist and the other for his hair as he stepped out and secured them around himself.

We proceeded to his dressing area, where I had his outfit for the day hanging with his briefs, tie, and shoes to match. He sat down, and I grabbed his coconut oil and rubbed it all through his scalp before I styled his locs. Once I finished with that, I began to moisturize his skin with frankincense scented shea butter. Then I moisturized his beard with a mixture of Jamaican black castor oil and amla oil and combed it through.

When I completed my ministrations, he stood to begin dressing. I picked up the discarded towels and then headed down to prepare his breakfast, which surprisingly was a light fare. Dominant required a smoothie with eggs and toast on the side. I grabbed the smoothie ingredients and whipped him up a green smoothie to keep him energized throughout his day. I plated his toast and eggs just as he sat down to the table.

Placing everything in front of him, I waited for him to try everything to make sure it was to his approval. He nodded his head, and I took a seat.

"How did you sleep last night?" Dominant asked me while he dug into his plate.

"I slept very well. The bed is a dream. Felt like I was sleeping on clouds."

"Very well, I'm glad you are finding your accommodations suitable."

"I am, and thank you again for thinking of me."

"No thanks needed. It's my job. I understand that you have to work, so I have arranged for my driver to pick you up and escort you to work. I'm only allowing you four days a week in the store physically. Thursdays and your weekends are exclusively mines. I have built you a workshop and office in one of the spare rooms so that you can be as creative as you need to be. You will call me once you are in the car and when you are leaving the store. Answer any text or correspondence from me throughout the day expeditiously. Are we understood?"

"Yes, daddy, I understand."

"Come see me off."

He stood, and I followed him to the door. I grabbed his briefcase from the wall hook before I handed him his belongings and made sure his clothes were lint free.

"Have a great day at work. See you tonight."

He bent down and kissed my cheek before heading out to work. I headed back upstairs to grab a little nap before it was time for me to go into the store. I made sure my phone was laying on the pillow next to me just in case he needed me. I drifted off, thinking that I could have never found an arrangement more perfect.

Chapter 13: Dominant

It had been a few weeks since I moved Kitten in, and our arrangement was a breath of fresh air. She made my mornings grand and nights enjoyable. I figured she was due for a reward. No woman had ever met all of my needs efficiently and with no hesitations, and that needed recognition.

Just last night, I was having a bad day. It was Thursday, and those were always bad for me. Last night was awful, thinking about my past. No matter how much I tried, I couldn't escape the demons. I got home, and as usual, she met me at the door with my favorite drink. She took my jacket and work bag and led me to the living room where she sat at my feet while I watched the news and unwound. I had no niceties for her, though. I barked and complained about every little thing. Her walking too slow, the television volume being too low, made her remake my drink four times when the first one was perfect. On the last round to get my drink, she took a little longer than usual.

Upon her return, she came with my favorite paddle. She apologized for making my life difficult then laid across my lap. That one action solidified my loyalty to her. That night, I spanked her until my body was exhausted, and my mind was clear. She never said a word the whole time, and when she noticed my dick was hard from the punishment, she got down and gobbled my dick up like she was starving. She snatched my kids right out my nuts and then laid on my lap and thanked me for using her to feel better. It got no better than that.

Ta'iah never questioned me about where my aggression came from on Thursdays. She would only offer me an outlet, and that's what I needed. So tonight, I was going to pamper her and reward her with some good dick. No, I had not had sex with her yet. Sex tended to make my subs soft, spoiled, and extremely difficult to manage. When it came to me, I had no time for entanglements. It was best if a woman saved her feelings for someone who needed them, because I didn't.

I pulled my phone out to text her, and as always, she responded right back.

Me: Tonight, I want you to go straight home and wait in your room until I come to get you.

My Lil Kitten: Yes daddy, have I done anything wrong?

Me: Don't ask questions follow directions

My Lil Kitten: I apologize I will be home directly

Me: Good girl I will see you tonight

I sat down at my desk and went through some emails until I noticed one from my brother. I opened it up and read that he and his wife would be coming to town with my niece and nephew as well as a surprise. This damn fool knew I hated surprises. I immediately grabbed my phone to call him.

"Yizzo, you finally remembered you had a brother." Justice was always in his feelings.

"Cut that soft shit out. I just got your email. What's up with the surprise visit?"

"A nigga can't miss his brother? Your sister-in-law has been on my ass about checking on you. She misses your reclusive ass too."

"Tell Pure that I'm good. She is not gon' make us kumbaya like her and her sister. My nuts hang low, not flat."

"Tell me yourself. Now what about your nuts?" This soft nigga put my sister-in-law on the phone, and I knew she was about to go off on me. Justice knew I didn't cut up in front of the ladies, so he pulled out the big guns.

"Awww man, P, I don't know what you're talking about. I was telling my brother that all is well, and you guys don't have to waste a trip here."

"Shut your lying ass up. You are always giving my baby shit. I know how you like your privacy and all that good shit, but we are your family. Family takes care of each other. Nobody has seen your ugly face in a year, and we are coming to check you out, so be your ass accommodating," Pure demanded after giving me an earful.

"If I'm ugly, then your husband's ugly."

"Boy, the lies you tell. My husband looks like a full course meal. I don't know where you got that leftover face. I keep trying to tell Justice y'all gotta be fraternal."

I busted out laughing at her simple ass. It was times like this that I missed having family around. Pure was the best sister-in-law a man could have. She was good for and to my brother. In an ordinary world, I would want one of her, but I wasn't wired that way.

"Sis, you're crazy. Tell your husband to send the itinerary over, and we can set something up. Oh yeah, what's the surprise?" I tried to slide that into the conversation since it was the primary reason for my call.

"I'm not telling you, or it wouldn't be a surprise. See you in a month or so, ugly."

"Alright, I forgot to mention I will have a houseguest, so please refrain from your shenanigans."

"*Shut up!* Dominant got a girlfriend. Babe, your brother got a girlfriend." I put my head in my palm. This girl always made a big deal out of anything.

"Bro, what is she talking about? Why you didn't tell me you had someone special."

"Bul, it's not that serious. You know I don't do girlfriends. It's not that deep, but since she will be in attendance, I will not act as if she is not a guest in my home."

"What the hell. Does she live there?" my brother asked me in a panic.

"For now."

"My mans, you live with a whole woman, and you're acting like it's not that serious."

"It doesn't matter. She is there, so don't make her feel awkward, and get your wife."

"You can get these nuts. My wife is perfect and harmless."

"Whatever, sensitive ass nigga. See you when you touch down."

After hanging up with the crazies, I grabbed my things and headed out. Tonight, I would beat Ta'iah home and get ready to take her on the ride of her life.

Chapter 14: Ta'iah

When I arrived home, there was a robe and a note laid out on the bed. I picked up the letter and read it.

Kitten,

Tonight, I intend to reward you for being a great student. You exceed my expectations. I have a few rules for tonight.

1. *No touching*

2. *No matter what takes place tonight our roles are still the same*

3. *Enjoy yourself because this is a privilege*

Place the robe on and meet me in my quarters in a half hour

After reading and then re-reading the note, I became emotional because pleasing him was easy. Dominant at times could be insufferable, mostly on Thursdays, but I'd found a way to reach him. I paid attention to every cue he gave me, and I followed obdurately, and that was because he deserved my submission. Dominant was a great leader, the best I'd ever had.

After a while, I undressed and donned the robe per his request. I didn't know what he had planned for me, but I would do just as he said and enjoy myself. I headed out of my room, and when I reached the door, I knocked gently. The few seconds I waited set my nerves on edge.

"Come in." Dominant's velvet-smooth voice came through the door, and it immediately put me at ease.

I walked into the room, and the lights were dim with candles lit around the room. Dominant stood before me in silk lounge pants that hung dangerously low on his hips. I made no moves toward him, only stood there and took it all in. I put my head down in reverence. The fact that he would take the time to make me feel special made him beatific in my eyes.

"Come to me, Kitten," he beckoned.

My feet moved of their own volition. For I was his to command. When I reached him, I stood there with my limbs relaxed as subservience radiated my whole being. He lifted my chin, but my eyes remained lowered beneath my lashes. A man of this much power could never be my equal. As he said, our roles were still the same.

"Do you like what I have set up for you?"

"Yes, thank you for finding me deserving."

"You are such a good girl. Even when being rewarded, you put my needs first." Why would I not when I knew that he needed my praise as much as I needed his leadership?

He kissed my forehead before grabbing my hand and leading me into the bathroom. I saw that he had a bath drawn in his whirlpool tub. Rose petals were floating in the water, and I didn't even know what to feel. In my mind, I was telling myself to calm down and enjoy the moment. But how could my heart not flutter at the care he took to do this for… me?

He came around the back of me and helped me to remove my robe and get into the tub. The water was the perfect temperature. At first, I sat there rigidly, afraid to move, afraid to breathe, and then I felt him gently begin to massage my shoulders.

"It's okay to relax, Kitten."

I released the breath I was holding and allowed my limbs to submerge in the water entirely. After a while, Dominant grabbed a loofah and told me to stand. Very gently, he started to wash my body. His strokes were as delicate as if he was handling a flower. Taking a pitcher, he filled it and rinsed my body. He repeated a few times before he helped me out of the bath and dried every inch of me.

We were back in his bedroom, where he went to his dresser and grabbed a bottle of oil. He uncapped the bottle and poured a generous amount in his hand before he rubbed me from my scalp down to my feet. The oil smelled divine and felt heavenly upon my skin as he deeply massaged every inch of me. Once he completed his task, he took a step back and perused me from head to toe.

"You're all oiled up and ready. That shit looks hot. Kneel on the bed, and place your face down."

I readily got onto the bed and put a deep arch in my back. I could hear Dominant moving around and drawers opening and closing. Then I felt his presence behind me. I started feeling excited and felt my body begin to vibrate with unspent energy.

"Be easy, Kitten. Your reward is coming. Now reach your hands behind your back and lie still."

When my hands were behind my back, he grabbed them and then crossed them at the wrist. Dominant proceeded to wrap a silky fabric around my right wrist. Once secured, I felt him tie it to my left ankle. Then he repeated the action, securing my left wrist to my right ankle. Dominant checked the knots to make sure they were secure.

"Hmmm, you look so lovely tied up like this. Tonight, I'm going to give you something that you have not had the pleasure of having. As long as you remember the rules, there may be a chance to get it again. Are we understood?"

"Yes." I felt a smack on my ass.

"Yes, what?"

"Yes, daddy, we are understood."

He then spread my legs apart widely. I felt his hands on my waist and then his lips upon my back. His tongue traveled up my spine before he placed a kiss between my shoulder blades. The feeling was so erotic and full of sensuality. Dominant's hands groped my ass, going between rubbing and light smacks.

He took his time like a predator stalking his prey. The anticipation had me delirious with passion. Being tied up was about trust, but it also left you vulnerable. That made the experience more intense—the uncertainty of what would happen or when it would happen, left one on the precipice of passion waiting to be tipped over.

Now his fingers strummed my love box, and I was beginning to leak. He would gradually increase the speed, and when I got close to erupting, he would slow down, only to start this process again, but this time, he alternated between strumming and dipping his fingers inside of me. I was leaking profusely, and I'm sure the aftermath on the sheets was indecent. Then he started to attack my clit vigorously, and as I approached orgasm, he slammed his dick inside of me. That first stroke robbed me of my breath and almost snatched my soul. Not only was he long, but he was thick and stretched me like no other, but I knew better than to cum without permission. He was not moving, just staying seated inside of me.

"I knew your walls would be perfection. Tonight, I'm going to own you completely. I will write my name all over this shit."

Dominant started slowly stroking me to a rhythm of in and out with a little swivel. His pace was teasing, almost antagonizing, but he was in control, always in control. Dominant's movements were unhurried, and it mimicked making love, but I was sure that this was not that. I let out an involuntary moan as I felt him tugging on the ties. He pulled my upper body up, and then he started fucking me hard. He was busting my pussy wide open, and I began to scream because the brutality in his stroke was making me certifiable.

"Shut up and cum on this dick, *now!*"

I closed my mouth and did just that. I was beyond exhausted, but I could tell that Dominant was far from done. He pulled out of me and then turned my body facing him. His tumescence was sitting in my face like the sweetest temptation, so I opened my mouth, ready to inhale him.

Smack!

"Close your mouth. You won't be getting off easy tonight. I'm about to make you ride this dick 'til that lil' pussy swole."

He got behind me and stretched my legs out as far as they would go. Dominant then placed his legs between mine and laid back. Maneuvering the scarves, he held me right over his dick and then began easing me down onto his dick. When I was fully seated, Dominant snatched my hair back and proclaimed.

"You better ride this dick as if your life depends on it. My cum is the prize, and you have to earn it."

Challenge accepted. When he let my hair go, I began gyrating on his length. I'd started a nice rhythm while I used my PC muscles to keep a good grip and my balance. Every up and down made my pussy tsunami wet.

"Just like that, Kitten. You are doing good, but you better make me believe you want this nut."

His encouragement was all I needed to let loose. I figured out a way to rise on my tippy toes and used the leverage to bounce on his dick like my name was Ms. Pogo. I was close to bursting. It was by far the best dick I'd ever had. I didn't think I could stop my orgasm.

"Daddy, may I have permission to cum?"

"Permission denied. There will be no cumming until I'm certain I own this shit."

Tears of frustration flowed down my cheeks because I wasn't disobedient. But his dick was touching places that had never been felt before, so my body's need to release was almost involuntary. He flipped us over again, never slipping out. Dominant placed his hand around my throat as he pulled my torso flush against his chest. He was bouncing me up and down, and I trembled from head to toe, trying to hold my orgasm. That's when he started whispering in my ear.

"This pussy fits me like a glove. Do you want me to own it?"

"Yes, daddy, it's yours."

"Are you sure it's mine?"

"Yesssss!"

"Well, understand this. The minute my nut blesses your womb, you will be ruined for any other. I don't give my nut freely, so you should show gratitude for this privilege. My cum means it's mine forever, because I don't share, and another will never be able to go into a place I made a home. Do you understand?"

"Yes, daddy."

"Now cum all over this dick and catch this nut."

I blasted off at the same moment he did. He pulled out and pushed me forward.

"That is such a perfect sight. My cum is dripping from your pretty pussy. I made the right choice."

I felt so good at that moment as he began to untie me. Dominant rubbed my wrist and ankles to help me gain circulation again. I felt myself getting drowsy, and my eyes drifted shut. He slapped my ass, and I jolted awake.

"Oh no, Kitten, there will be no sleeping. It's going to be a long night. I'm about to fill you with so much cum you will never be hungry again."

And a long night it was. The first of many.

Chapter 15: Ta'iah

I had been cooking all day preparing for the arrival of Dominant's guests. Dominant gave me a specific menu of all of their favorites. I'd cooked seven cheese baked penne, fried silver trout, pasta salad, a summer salad, yeast rolls, and sweet cornbread. For dessert, I reached out to a local bakery to get cupcakes and a sweet potato cheesecake.

While my fish fried, I became lost in thought. True to his words, our roles did not change. Although, he had been doing things out of the norm like chilling and watching Netflix and making me sleep in his room so I didn't have to walk far to start our daily routine. He even began asking me about myself and essential things, although he never shared about himself. Lately, I'd started to wonder what our relationship would become if it were conventional.

When my heart started to get away from me, I would remind myself there was room for nothing but our roles. It was easy for our lines to get crossed since we had become cozy with one another. All I could do was swallow my feelings and use my imagination to explore the what ifs. Dominant has genuinely ruined me for anyone else in more ways than one.

After making this last batch of fish, I had about twenty minutes before Dominant made it home and about thirty minutes before his guests arrived. I took a quick shower and placed the outfit on that he specified for me to wear. It was a long, black maxi dress with some gladiator sandals. Simple yet sexy, and my hair was in a high bun. I added some wooden accessories, and I was ready to go.

Just as my foot hit the last step, I heard his key in the door. Rushing to the foyer to meet him, I grabbed the nightcap I'd placed there before I took a shower. When he walked in, I quickly admired the way he wore a suit. Dominant turned his back to me, and I assisted him with taking his jacket off. I picked his drink up and handed it to him. He bent down, and I put my cheek against his, rubbing it affectionately, then he placed a kiss on my forehead.

"How was your day, Kitten?"

"It was well. Everything has been prepared to your specifications."

"That's good. I am going to change into something more comfortable. Do you remember what I told you about tonight?"

"Yes, I remember everything you have instructed."

"Let me hear it again just to be sure."

"I am to appear as a close associate but not a girlfriend. I'm to appear affectionate but not overly so. I must please you without your family knowing the true dynamics of our relationship. I can interact with your guests, but personal things should be deferred to you for approval on what is to be answered. Most of all, I am to make your guests feel at home."

"Good girl. I know that I can count on you to see to this happening without a hitch."

"Yes, always."

"I will be back down in just a sec. Make sure to do the last check on everything."

I went and made sure everything was placed in its appropriate pan. Then, I'd set everything out buffet style. I checked to make sure the place settings were all straight, and then I waited at the bottom of the steps for Dominant to return.

I heard him ascending just as the doorman called up to let us know our guests had arrived. He grabbed my hand,

and I smiled demurely at him as we headed to the elevators to greet his guests. We heard the ding of the elevator's arrival. Soon as the doors opened, this short and voluptuous woman launched herself at Dominant. Her antics had Dominant laughing heartily, and I felt slightly jealous because I'd never elicited that response from him.

"Brother, oh my God! It feels good to lay these 20/20's on ya."

"Sis, you are crazy as hell. Get down before I have to beat your husband's ass," he told the little lady.

"Nigga, you wish you would beat my ass. And ya damn sure better put my wife down. Come on, bring it in."

Dominant was laughing from his soul, and it looked good to see him so relaxed. His brother was his twin, just without the locs. You could measure the love they had for each other as they stood there talking with their foreheads touching. I saw an older couple standing off to the side. Dominant was so wrapped up in his brother's embrace that he must not have noticed them until the older gentlemen cleared his throat.

"It's good to see you, son. Can I get some of that love?"

"Papa…" He started to say, but then he looked to the man's right and noticed the woman with him. She stood there wearing one of the evilest smiles I'd ever seen. Dominant pulled the older gentleman in for a warm embrace. When he turned to the woman, he was stuck in place.

"What's the matter, boy? You not happy to see your family?" Dominant grabbed my hand and was squeezing it extra tight. He didn't utter one word to her. I looked into his eyes, and I saw pain, but it was quickly replaced with a vacant look. Who the hell was this woman, because I'd

never seen him like this before.

Chapter 16: Dominant

I couldn't move, and my heart was beginning to panic. It had been years since I saw my grandparents. I spoke to my Papa all the time, but not as often as I should. Too many memories flitted through my mind, and it felt like I was sinking. I needed an anchor, and Ta'iah was close. When I grabbed her hand, I automatically relaxed. Her comfort was all I needed to shut my emotions down and put my mask in place.

"Twin, are you good?"

"Yeah, Justice, I'm fine. You didn't tell me Papa was your guest."

"Papa and Nan missed you, so Pure thought it would be a good idea to surprise you with them. It has been at least ten years—"

"Twelve years." I cut him off with the exact number.

"However many it was, it has been way too long. We are all we got," Justice replied

Whatever he said at that point didn't matter. I could hear him, but I didn't feel him. Justice would never understand why this unexpected visit was bothering me. No one would ever know. I would not fold. I pulled Ta'iah to the front and began introductions.

"This is Ta'iah, a close companion of mine."

"She is just so cute. Come here, girl, and hug me." You would swear Pure was raised in the south with her hospitality. Ta'iah looked to me for approval, and I subtly nodded, and she walked into Pure's arms. While they were embracing, I looked at my Papa's wife, and she had excitement in her eyes, looking like an evil vulture, and I hated that. *Let's get this night over with, so I can get back to my routine.*

"Ta'iah can you escort everyone to the table so we can eat while it's hot."

"Sure, of course. Everybody right this way."

She led them to the dining room, and I took my seat at the head of the table. Ta'iah fixed my plate first then waited for me to nod my approval. She then poured me a drink and then proceeded to make her plate. My family was looking at her curiously, but no one addressed her mannerisms. We started eating in silence when my papa broke the silence.

"Your home is beautiful, son. You have been doing alright for yourself since you left the nest, I see." Papa complimented me, and it felt good to have his approval, especially since he had never been in my personal space.

"Humph..." His wife made a noise, which she tried to mask in a cough. My Papa started patting her back.

"You okay, dear?"

"Yes. Girl, go and fetch me some water." I knew she was addressing Ta'iah. Ta'iah looked at me with wide eyes, and I shook my head no, and she relaxed.

"She will not. There are drinks on the table as the food is spread out buffet style." I shut Papa's wife down.

"Oh, I see the only one here able to get served is you, huh?" I didn't even respond to her. Pure must've sensed the tension, so she tried to mediate the situation.

"I will get you the water if it's all the same to you." Pure offered a compromise.

"You will not. That girl can get it. Now," his wife stated while looking at Ta'iah sternly. Ta'iah snapped to attention as she could feel her dominance. She looked at me in distress, and I shook my head no, which caused her to stop eating and put her hands in her lap and bow her head. That shit pissed me smooth off.

"Ta'iah is my guest. *Mine!* And she will serve no one. She has done enough with the preparations today. Ta'iah, eat." She picked her fork right up and commenced to eating.

"Justice, what's new on the scene in Atlanta?" I asked my brother as a way to divert the crisis that was happening in the room.

"Everything is everything. Signed a few new clients, and Pure even found what she calls her Pen Soulmate." That was all Justice needed to say for Pure to start telling us all about this poet La-La, who not only wrote poetry but could sing and write songs. She seemed like a great asset to the label. I would be the judge of that once I saw her work.

Even with Pure regaling us with stories, it did nothing to soothe the atmosphere. The mood was strained and heavy. Even with the forced chatter, the tension didn't dissipate by much.

Eventually, everyone finished with their meal, and we retired to the living room. Ta'iah left to grab dessert and asked everyone what drinks they would like with dessert. After bringing the dessert, drinks, and cups, everyone started serving themselves.

Pure was in my brother's lap while they were whispering to each other. My Papa and his wife were sitting on the couch. Ta'iah brought our dessert over and then sat between my legs. She placed her head in my lap, and I took her bun down. I loved to play in Ta'iah's hair because it soothed me. We were all just enjoying the moment when Pure started talking, and it went from sugar to shit real quick.

"You two are so darn cute. I am looking at two generations of love around the room. I'm going to hate that we all are leaving you guys here. It would be good to have everyone together all the time in Atlanta." I thought I heard her, but I needed to make sure that I had my facts straight.

"How would we all be together in Atlanta when four of us live here?" I looked around the room, and when they landed on my Papa's wife, she was looking so smug, but what she said next triggered all of my pent-up anger

"Oh boy, you didn't know we will be moving in with Justice and Pure next week. She needs help with the baby since he is not school age. While they travel on tour. You know I love my grandkids, especially my grandsons." Then she sat back with a self-satisfied smirk because I caught her drift. Now she was about to catch mine. Her covert perversity broke the dam on my pent-up feelings

"You evil bitch, you only wanna go babysit because your ass is sick in the head and the heart. It doesn't have shit to do with love and everything to do with your degradation. I can see that insane look in your eyes. What, are you planning to go fuck him too? Not while I'm living and breathing. I will end your miserable fucking life before I ever allow you to do to him what you did to me." Pure gasped, and I knew I was vulgar, but I couldn't let her evil destroy another generation.

I never noticed getting up, but I was pacing back and forth, and everything just started flashing through my mind.

The old lady in front of me was my molester and rapist. She did things to me that no woman should ever do to a child. Just the thought of her going anywhere near my nephew was making me sick. Justice jumped in my path, and I almost ran him over in my pacing. Justice was looking at me questioningly. I shook my head no, indicating I didn't want to talk about it. He pulled me in close and stared into my eyes while our foreheads touched. I held his gaze as tears silently fell down my face.

I had to get out of there because the walls were closing in, and my control was slipping. I couldn't function in this headspace, and I couldn't even look at Ta'iah.

I left the room because now that my biggest secret was public knowledge, I felt my armor slip. They say a man ain't supposed to cry. We were supposed to be strong. I didn't know how I could anymore.

Chapter 17: Ta'iah

It was sheer pandemonium as I watched Dominant slowly break down. My heart was screaming to get up and comfort him someway somehow. Still, I knew after losing his emotions in front of his family, he didn't need a reminder of his moment of weakness. Dominant needed to remain steadfast in front of them. I watched as his brother grabbed him close, and they communicated silently. Then Dominant stormed out of the room. My heart desired to run after him, but I was frozen in place as the drama continued unfolding.

"Nan, what the hell is my brother talking about?" Justice asked their grandmother.

"That boy was just talking. Don't be asking me questions about shit."

"Nah, I know my twin, and whatever happened is affecting him, and I want to know."

"I don't fucking answer to you. That boy is just a little pussy like always, with his scary, dramatic ass. All those damn theatrics and crying like a lil' bitch and running out the room. Should call his little ass Dominita." Who was this woman? She was such a bitch, and I was about ready to put my hands on her.

Justice lunged for his grandmother, but Pure intercepted him and held him in place. That old hag just started laughing as if she was amused by the chaos she created.

"Shirley, I know that I'm a little older now, but I think that I understand that my grandson just said you were raping him." He looked to us as if for confirmation that it was what Dominant said, and we all nodded affirmingly.

"You ol' fool, that boy didn't say none of the sort. What type of God-fearing woman would do the things that you are claiming? A heathen I tell you. I won't have you or anybody tell lies on my good name." Their grandfather only looked at her, and then he started speaking to himself as he paced.

"No, it makes sense. I remember that their father told me that you used to mess with him, and I beat my son's ass for even saying such things about the woman who held him in his womb. I remember that after that day, he stopped coming home. I would only see him when you were not around, and he never brought my grandsons to see us unless at a huge family event. Yeah, now it all makes sense."

He seemed to be having an internal battle, trying to piece this puzzle together. Then the tears started pouring out of his eyes, and it caused us all to start crying. Nobody could ever imagine the things that went on under their very own roof. I could see the turmoil he was facing at feeling like he didn't protect his son nor his grandson.

"You are talking crazy, you damn fool. Your son was a liar, and his son is a liar. That's why I couldn't stand either one of them. We are not about to keep talking about this when nothing I have done has hurt either one of them. I loved them the most, and now they want to act like I'm the bad guy. I am ready to go."

What she said halted their grandfather midstride. I didn't think she realized she'd just admitted to what they accused. They said anger would make a fool speak the truth. Before anybody could blink, their grandfather had his hands around his wife's throat and yoked her out her chair.

"You're a sick bitch! You would admit that shit to me casually as if your actions have not broken two generations of men. I loved my son and lost him because you couldn't contain your evil. You don't understand it's not natural for a woman to lay with her son, let alone her grandson. I won't lose my grandson. I will put you in a ditch first, bitch!"

He was choking her so hard her wig was sliding as she clawed at his hands. Justice was trying to remove his hands, but their grandfather was determined to end her life.

"Papa, let her go… please." His grandfather shook her and then dropped her on the floor as if she was trash. He stood there crying, and I saw him begin to massage his chest. Then he looked as if he had been electrocuted and started clutching his chest as if in pain, and then he passed out.

I rushed in and checked his breathing, and it was shallow, as was his pulse. I began performing CPR on him as Justice called the paramedics. Pure approached their grandmother and let her have it.

"I am not for disrespecting my elders, but your ass gotta go. The turmoil you caused this family is enough for a lifetime. I will call you an Uber, and once we figure out what's wrong with Papa Holloway, then we will let him decide what to do with you." She said that while grabbing the lady's wig and dragging her to the elevator.

As she was leaving out, the paramedics were coming in. I would think their grandmom would have protested, but like the coward she was, she just left.

They began working on their grandfather and loaded him onto a stretcher to take him to the hospital. I didn't know what to do or where to help. I just stood there, and before I knew it, Pure came to wrap her arms around me.

"It will be okay. You do your best to take care of my brother. I have a feeling that you are very important, even if he doesn't realize it."

I could only hope that she was right because I had a feeling nothing would ever be the same again.

Chapter 17: Dominant

My world and everything in it had come crashing

down. I worked so hard to leave what happened to me in

the past. I was so frustrated because, as a man, it was hard

to be transparent when you were taught to conceal

emotions. You were expected to grab your nuts and just

live with the pain. You damn sure better not ever talk about

it, or you would be viewed as weak. All the years of

suppressing my hurt had finally built enough pressure to

burst.

When I looked into my abuser's eyes as she

mentioned my nephew, it was the same disgusting look she

had for me. That look led to evil so vile that its perversity broke my manhood. It was as if she couldn't wait to prey again. At that moment, I knew my silence would continue to be part of the problem. I needed to be a part of the solution.

I stood in my bathroom, staring in the mirror, and it was as if I didn't see the man I'd become. My reflection was that of the boy I once was. All the pain came rushing back. I thought about the first time she touched me.

We had only been with our grandparents for two weeks. We had buried our parents the week before, and it was hard on us both. Justice was having a hard time adjusting to sleeping in separate areas because until we moved there, we had never been separated. My nan had split us up, saying it was unnatural for boys our age to share a room still, so she made room for me in the basement, and his room was on the second floor with them.

We were chilling in my room, and Justice was making beats on the table while I studied for my Calculus test.

We were talking about what we wanted for our lives after jail, as we called living at our grandparent's house. Justice was telling me all about how he was going to be the hottest producer on the east coast. He told me how I was going to run his company as the brains, and he would be the face. In the middle of us shooting the shit, my nan called downstairs.

"Cut out all that racket. It's time for bed."

"Uggghh, I can't wait to leave here," Justice told me.

"Twin, it's not that bad. We just have to adjust. In four years, we are out of here. We can make it," I assured him

"I just miss Mama and Daddy so much. It's hard realizing they are never coming back." I got off my chair and pulled him into my arms and placed my forehead on

his and just stared at him. We had done this for each other as comfort since we were small.

"Listen, I miss them too. They taught us to weather any storm. As long as I'm breathing and beyond that, I got you. I promise. We are all we got, and it's us against the world." That seemed to calm him down. We hugged and parted ways.

When he left, I jumped in the shower and prepared for bed. I don't even think I slept for an hour when it felt like my penis was wrapped in something tight and wet. I had never been touched sexually, so I knew I had to be dreaming.

In health class, they told us about wet dreams, and I was sure this was it. That was until I heard moaning, and it made me wake up out of my daze. I looked down and saw that it was my nan and tried to move her off me.

"Nan, what..." My words were cut off when she jumped up and clamped her hand down on my mouth.

"Shut your ass up. Nobody asked you to speak."

She was my elder, and I felt compelled to obey her. She

kept feeling on me almost admiringly. The look in her eyes

was a mixture of excitement and predatory.

"You were walking around my house with this big

ol' dick on display. Coming in with your shirt off, looking

like you wanted me to touch you. I knew you were teasing

me, inviting me to come and get a taste." Her words were

repulsing me, and it caused me to cry.

"What are you crying for, boy? You've been

begging for this." She removed her hand from my mouth

and moved both hands down to caress my penis. I was a

virgin, and it felt good, but I knew it was bad, and that

made me cry harder. I decided to try and plead with her.

"Nan, please! I don't want to do this. It is not

right." She turned to look me dead in my eyes and laughed

maniacally.

"You lil' bitch. Sitting here crying like you're afraid to get your manhood taken. Let me tell you this. I'm not only going to take your manhood, but I am going to break you. I'm going to mold you into my proper pet. Everything you learn will be at my hands, and you will remember how special this time was. Now, either you're going to give it to me, or I will go and take it from your precious brother. So, what's it going to be, bitch?" The thought of her doing this to my brother damn near broke me. I had to protect him, and if it meant playing these sick games, then I would be the M.V.P. I sucked my tears up and stopped resisting her.

"Good boy." Then she proceeded to violate me orally. All night, she fucked and sucked me, and that was the routine for four years. Every damn Thursday, I was hers.

I shook off the memories and then punched the mirror repeatedly until my image became distorted. In the cracks, I saw Ta'iah standing behind me. The last thing I needed was her bearing witness to my meltdown. How could I be what she needed me to be if I was broken inside?

Without saying anything, Ta'iah went under the cabinet and grabbed the first aid kit. She ran my hands under cold water to stop the blood flow. Looking at my hands to assess my wounds, she then grabbed the tweezers. Tenderly she plucked the glass from my injuries in silence. Afterward, she used peroxide to disinfect my wounds before putting ointment on them and wrapping my hands.

She stood there so submissive, demure, and willing. Had I been in my right mind frame, I would have enjoyed it because subservience looked good on her. For the first time in my life, I felt undeserving. Unsuitable was a new feeling, and it was making me lose control.

"Daddy, I don't know what you need from me, but whatever it is, I can be."

It almost caused me to reach out and hug her. Tell her I needed comfort because I longed for it deep inside, but because of that depraved bitch, I didn't know how to express my feelings safely without feeling judgment or relinquishing control. And that thought alone caused me to get angry all over again. I had to do something I knew would break Ta'iah, but it became necessary at this point.

"Ta'iah eyes up," I commanded, and she snapped to attention.

"There is nothing else you can do for me. Effective immediately, our contract is void."

Her eyes got wide, and she fell to her knees

"Please don't do this. What have I done? Please tell me, and I will fix it. Just please don't separate from me. Please reconsider."

Tears were pouring from her eyes, and for the first time in my life, I hated myself. I didn't know how to address her emotions. I didn't want to separate from her, but her needs were specific, and after tonight, I was uncertain if I could fulfill that need. My life as I knew it would never be the same again.

"Ta'iah, I will not reconsider. This arrangement is over."

I just left out of the bathroom. Seeing Ta'iah on her knees, willing to be whatever I needed was too much for my heart to take. I raced downstairs, and my house was empty and in disarray. I stopped in the foyer and grabbed my keys, before getting on the elevator. In the parking garage, I hopped in my car and jumped straight on the road.

I had quite a drive ahead of me to get to my secret spot. I shot my brother a text letting him know I was going underground. He knew what that meant and how to reach me if I was needed. He responds, letting me know that they were in the hospital with Papa and that he would keep me updated. I needed to go clear my head and deal with what had become of my life.

Chapter 18: Justice

It had been a few days since my brother texted me he was going underground. He hadn't done that since right before we went off to college. No one would ever know how heartbroken I was for my twin. Those revelations rocked us as a family. My brother had never been overly emotional, so watching him cry was like being stabbed in the heart repeatedly.

I thought back to that time we spent in my grandparents' home. I saw the change but didn't know what to attribute it to. He always made sure that I was never alone with Nan. He made sure to discuss sex with me and even to tell him if someone was messing with me. I thought he was overprotective. You couldn't have paid me ever to believe that those types of things happened in black families, so I never took what he said seriously.

Around college time, I noticed that he became very private. Not that he ostracized me or anything, but more so in how he moved. I never saw him date, and college was the time where we spread our wild oats. I even questioned if my brother was a switch hitter to which he laughed from the bottom of his belly. I mean, I just wanted to know because it would not have changed anything. I just needed to know if when he brought Anna home, was she gon' have a little extra bass in her voice. He assured me that he was very much so straight, but he liked to keep his dating life private. He assured me that the only woman he would bring home was his wife.

I let him rock because as long as he was good, I was good. Now I wish he would have let me in on what he went through. Knowing Dominant, he took his role as protector seriously. He was not even the oldest, but that was the role he naturally assumed. He would rather cut off his right arm than see me hurt. He always took the burden on himself. It was a blessing but a curse as well.

"Babe, you about ready to go?" my beautiful wife Pure asked me

"Yes, I'm ready, beautiful."

No matter how many times I complimented her, she still blushed. To think, at one time, I wasn't there to place those blushes on her cheeks. It was a time when our love was tested, and I was thankful every day that love was able to redeem us, and our sad song became a Pure Melody.

We headed out of our hotel, toward the Hospital of the University of Pennsylvania to visit my Papa. That night of the dinner, he suffered a mild heart attack. They had been keeping him for observation, and today was release day, so we were headed up to the hospital to pick him up.

We were driving, and I was so thankful for a loving and supportive wife. Pure had held me when I cried for my brother and didn't judge me or make me feel awkward. She had talked me through my feelings and given me the best advice. She was my rib for sure. She fit me perfectly.

We got to the hospital and took the elevator up to the cardiac floor. Once we were on the floor getting closer to Papa's room, we heard raised voices. We rushed to the door and walked in on my grandparents arguing.

"I don't understand what you mean by you're moving to Georgia, and we are getting a divorce." I guess he couldn't wait to deliver that news. He was adamant about leaving Nan, and I stood with Papa in anything. So when he said he wanted to move out of state and divorce his wife, of course my wife and I opened our doors to him.

"There is nothing to explain. If you think that I would ever lay with a woman who has broken the innocence and the pride of two men I love with my being, you gotta be bat shit crazy."

"So you just say fuck forty-five years of marriage because them bastards lied on me? You're not getting a divorce. I don't care what you feel."

"I wish it was a lie. *Two men!* Ones that were the better part of me, and it was my job as the patriarch to protect, teach, capture, and cultivate them into worthy men. And I failed miserably. To think that the woman I loved and chose to give my essence to hold in her womb to help build a legacy would tarnish it. A legacy I thought we built on our foundation of love and honor. A woman that was supposed to protect that legacy and help build an empire. But no, she used the same womb that housed kings to tear that legacy down. You are the worst of individuals. And I'm disgusted that it took me damn near half a century to figure that out."

"All you ever cared about was your son. Then when he married that girl and had not one but two sons, it was like they hung the stars and moon. How did you expect me to feel when I knew I couldn't compete?" She sounded crazy, and Papa told her as much.

"That was the dumbest shit I ever heard. I was their father. I was supposed to uplift my son so that he, in turn, could uplift his. I was proud to know that even when I was dead and gone, at least everything I taught them would live on, and that is the true completion of life. You are trying to tell me that because you were jealous that I gave them their birthright, it made you not only fuck your son but his son too. You're about a dizzy bitch. That is why I won't waste another moment of my life on you. You don't even think what you did was wrong." He looked to her, and for the first time, I saw my nan drop tears.

"I can't see anything wrong with it. It was done to me, and I was told it was normal. When I told my pain, the adults gave me stories that happened to them, and it was just a special relationship. I didn't think that it would hurt them that bad. I thought I was showing them love." Damn, still waters ran deep.

"That makes me sad because no one deserves being preyed upon. Had you told me this, I could have helped you with your issues before those issues bled out and ruined my family. Communication is everything in a family. What doesn't get discussed can never be healed. You internalized it and allowed it to warp your sense of reality. I will never forgive you for what you did. There ain't no two ways about it. We are finished. Now please leave so that I can go home to my family and try to repair what is broken."

Nan just stared at Papa in disbelief for a moment. Then you saw the moment she resigned herself to her fate. She grabbed her things and left without a word to anybody. As soon as the door closed behind her, I heard my Papa let out the most gut-wrenching wail I'd ever heard. No man should ever have to face this battle he'd just met. I didn't know his pain, and may I never know it. Because to be this broken had to be the pits. I didn't think my heart would survive it, and I just prayed that his heart could.

"Son, how do I fix this? My grandson looked so broken. I owe it to him to make it right. I would have never allowed her to do that to him. I would have taken you boys and left. You have to believe me. I won't rest until it is right." Papa was causing me to cry, and that, in turn, made Pure cry. There were no words for the sight before me. No man wanted to feel like a failure.

"Papa, we will get through it together. That's what families do. We got each other."

"I gotta get to your brother. I don't want him to feel like he is alone. He has dealt with this by himself for far too long." Papa was out of the bed and dressing hurriedly.

"He is not home, Papa. He went to a place that only he and I know about. He needs to clear his head."

"Well, if he is there, that's where I wanna be." I knew that feeling of wanting to be close to those you loved, but I knew my brother.

"Papa, I understand where you are coming from, but I know my brother, and he needs a minute to process everything that has happened. He will want to do that alone. I promise you we will give it no longer than a week and go see him, and no matter how long it takes, we will bring him back whole."

"That's fine, son. Has anyone checked on his lady friend?" Until Papa asked, I had forgotten that we left his lady all by herself.

"No, Papa. With everything that has been going on, it slipped our head. Let's check out of the hotel and head over to his house, because I know that she has to be going through it. I have a feeling she is important to him."

We gathered all of Papa's things, and when they brought him his discharge papers, we headed out. *Operation Bring My Brother Home* was in full effect.

Chapter 19: Ta'iah

He left me. The night of the dinner party was the day my world came crashing down on me. Never had I ever envisioned that he would terminate our contract. When he left, I stayed in my spot on the floor. My tears and anguish were met with the deafening silence of Dominant's home missing his presence.

All night, I sat there and just cried, afraid to move—afraid to face the end of all that my happiness had become. I knew he was going to come back in and say he overreacted. I just knew that he'd made a mistake. I sat there and thought and thought about what I could have done to make him make such a drastic decision.

I was perfect for him. Whatever he needed, I became pliable. I'd never asked for more than what he gave me, and honestly, I was content. So why was I here all alone? My brain did not compute.

With the rising of the sun, my denial was still evident. I jumped up and began cleaning up the house. For hours on end, I cleaned the house from top to bottom. I was reminding myself that he would not like to come home to a house in chaos. Then I had someone come replace the mirror in the bathroom so he'd have no reminders of the night that caused him so much pain. Nope, it would be as if it never happened. To me, that moment changed everything, so we would act as if it never happened.

I'd gone to my room to don one of his favorite dresses and put on his preferred scent and went to meet him at the door. I stood there attentively, waiting for his 5:30 p.m. arrival. Five thirty became 6:30 p.m., and before I blinked my eyeballs, the grandfather clock struck midnight. I was in utter disbelief, but I stood firm in my convictions.

At around 3 a.m., the tears began to fall, and I laid at the bottom of the stairs for a day, just letting my tears flow.

When I rose off of the floor, I finally accepted that he was not coming back. Our routine had been the same for months now. The newness of the broken arrangement was something I had a hard time processing.

I headed upstairs and got in Dominant's bed and just lay there. That is where I had been for the last four days. I couldn't eat, couldn't move, and sleep had been ever elusive. I grabbed my phone and, for the hundredth time, sent him a text message.

Big Zaddy: I don't know how I can go on without your guidance. You have become as essential to me as air. Your absence is overwhelming me. I could have never asked for a better teacher. You truly get me and my needs, and I need you to tell me what to do. I am begging you to please come back home and let's continue with the life we built. It was perfect for both of us. Daddy, please

reconsider. I will always need you!!!

I waited for a reply that never came. I knew Dominant wouldn't respond, and it had been a game I played with myself since getting in this bed. Texting him and waiting and then repeating the cycle.

While I was lying there in this dark room staring at the walls, I had an Aha moment. I remembered that his brother and sister-in-law are here in town, and I knew that they were business partners. If they were in town, I was sure they would be working from Dominant's office. Dominant wasn't there because I called and was told that he was on an indefinite hiatus. Why did I not think of this before?

My limbs got a burst of energy at the thought that his family would be able to lead me to Dominant. I could finally get the opportunity to plead my case in person. I hopped up out of bed with my body buzzing with excitement at our possible reunion.

I headed into the shower and scrubbed my body from head to toe like four times. Grabbing a razor, I shaved my vagina, underarms, and legs. I was grooming because I needed to be perfect to sway his mind. I would not take no for an answer. When I got out of the shower, I headed to the mirror, and I saw that my eyes were a bit puffy. Yikes, I would have to use a little more make-up then I liked but anything for him.

I sat at my vanity and started applying my shea butter all over my body. After that, I began to detangle and comb my hair from ends to root. Once I finished, I applied Knatural Kreations Smooth Repair Cream and brushed my hair up into a high curly ponytail.

In my room, I picked out a long, flowing sleeveless maxi dress and put it on. I added silver accents and headed to the mirror, and I appeared refreshed. I grabbed my tote bag and headed to our drawer to grab a few playthings. I'd picked up the oil, a collar, a gag with the hole in it, and his favorite paddle. I intended to pull out all of the tricks to remind him he needed me as much as I needed him.

After packing our toys, I got my wallet, keys, and phone and threw them in the bag before leaving the room. As I descended the stairs, I began to feel woozy. I tried to shake it off. My lightheadedness had to come from my lack of appetite, so I shrugged it off and pushed through the feeling.

By the time I got to my fourth step down, my vision got blurry. I reached out for the railing to try to still myself. When I almost grabbed it, my head started to spin and feel heavy, which caused me to slip. I was falling, and then everything went black.

Chapter 20: Pure

Wow, being in Philadelphia had been an adventure for sure. We never expected to be faced with so much adversity, but we were family, and together we could face anything. As I looked over at my husband, I fell in love all over again. He was my best friend, my lover, and my king. I knew that he was overwhelmed, but what was a wife if she couldn't share in the burden? I would hold him up when he felt like he was falling. I would be his anchor when he felt like he was drowning. No matter how hard or how deep, he would never have to face things alone.

My mind drifted to Dominant. My heart truly hurt for him. That man had suffered through so much and did it alone. He may have thought that he was broken, but I knew different. Dominant was bright, a wiz with numbers, and the reason our company made money hand over fist. He held his family up, and not for the fame, but because he genuinely loved them. Our children love their uncle D, and he and my daughter had such a strong bond, and it was surreal. He protected them as if they were his, and now I understood why he was so fierce in his duty to them.

We decided to go to Larry's to grab a cheesesteak and fries for us as a family. I could only imagine what Ta'iah was going through. We intended to comfort her as we comforted each other. After witnessing our craziness, we could not call her anything other than family.

When I met her that night, I thought that she was so beautiful. Her eyes were chinky and expressive and made you wonder at her heritage. Her skin was a smooth caramel complexion, and she had the wildest mane of curls I had ever seen. What got me the most was the way that she looked at him with such adoration. I wasn't even sure Dominant knew the extent of her feelings.

Her mannerisms were unlike anything I ever saw. She was not loud or overbearing in speech. Ta'iah served him like a king, and it didn't seem forced. It looked as natural as inhaling and exhaling. I hoped she wasn't put off by the spectacle that took place in her presence. The way she jumped into action when Papa Holloway passed out made me believe she was built Ford tough, and she would fit into our family.

"What you over there so deep in thought about, baby girl?" my husband asked me.

"Nothing, just hoping that Ta'iah is alright and up for company."

"I think she will be fine with having us there. I can only imagine how lonely she is without my brother there."

"You're right, babe. I think I can get her excited about having us there despite the circumstances."

"You sure can, granddaughter. Your happiness is infectious," Papa said to me, and his words made me smile.

"Oh, thank you, Papa. It's easy to be this happy when you are this loved." My husband gazed at me with the cheesiest grin on his face.

"Eyes on the road, mister. I'm trying to make it to my new sister in one piece," I reminded him as we are driving.

Twenty minutes later, we were parking. We exited our car and grabbed the food we bought and headed over to the elevator. We all got inside the elevator and rode up to the top floor. I was getting excited to have another girl around, and I hoped Ta'iah felt the same.

When we stepped off the elevator, it was eerily quiet. It was a little dark for it to be in the afternoon. I headed into the living room to open the drapes, and Justice went to find the lights. I think that the poor child was still in bed. Ta'iah was probably sick out of her mind with Dominant gone. That made me rush to the stairs so I could let her know that she had a family to help her deal with this.

When I reached the stairs, I saw Ta'iah lying in a heap at the bottom of the steps with her body at a weird angle. I began screaming. Justice and Papa came rushing to my side. I was checking for a pulse and assessing her injuries, but I didn't move her.

Ta'iah had a nasty knot on the side of her head. I just hoped that her injuries were minor. Now I felt like shit because she shouldn't have had to be here alone. We were all so wrapped up in our lives that we forgot about the poor child. That thought made me cry.

Then I heard the paramedics entering the house. They asked for her name, and I remembered her pocketbook was lying next to her. I opened the bag and rummaged around for her wallet. My hand hit leather, but when I pulled it out, it was a whip. What in the freakiness? I couldn't dwell on that now. I found the wallet and gave them her full name, age, and date of birth. I moved out of the way so the paramedics could do their job. My husband came over and wrapped me up in his arms, and I was glad for his comfort.

They told us they were taking her to Jefferson, and we prepared to head out after them. Papa decided to stay behind and stated he was tired. We hugged him on our way out and promised to keep him updated.

We rushed down to the car, trying to make sure we weren't too far behind the ambulance. I was shaking so bad that I dropped the keys. Justice picked the keys up and then placed his arms around me to settle me.

"Babe, calm down. Everything will be okay."

"I know. It's just been one thing after the other. Dom leaves, Papa has a heart attack, and now Ta'iah is in the hospital."

"I know, boo, but we are still standing tall. We're going to the hospital to be there for Ta'iah. We have to take it one step at a time."

"That's why I love you. You always know how to make me feel better."

Now we were headed over to Jefferson, which was only about five minutes away from the condo. We pulled up to the hospital and rushed inside the emergency room. I ran straight to the front desk.

"We are looking for my sister Ta'iah Harden. She was brought in by ambulance."

"Hold on one moment, ma'am." The nurse began typing on the computer and looking for Ta'iah. Then, her face dropped, and my heart started racing.

"It says here that she was rushed into surgery. You guys can head up to the operating floor and wait there in the family room. The elevators are down the hall to your right, and it's on the sixth floor."

We thanked her and headed up to the operating floor. I was a ball of nerves. I didn't know what to do about our current predicament. We made it to the family waiting area, and the silence was deafening. The void in the room made you feel like any news would be bad news. I sat down, and the gravity of the situation was wearing on me.

"Have you tried to reach Dom?" I ask my husband

"Yeah, I've been calling him since I got off the phone with dispatch. Still no answer."

"Just great! That poor girl probably needs him, and he is unavailable. I just hope she pulls through."

"Come on, babe. Don't begin to think negatively. He is not here, but we are, and we are going to wish for the best concerning our sister back there."

Justice was right. We couldn't let negative thoughts consume us as we waited on an excellent report from the doctor. It was time to get things in order. I'd arranged for a manager to come and take over Dom's duties in our Philadelphia office. After sending out emails and making sure everything was right in the Atlanta office and with our children, I was tired. I laid my head on my husband's shoulder and rested my eyes. I hadn't been getting much sleep because we'd been running since we got to Philly.

Before I could close my eyes good, the doctor entered the room. She was an older woman looking to be in her mid-fifties. Slim stick with cocoa-colored skin with salt and pepper hair pulled into a chignon at the nape of her neck.

"Family of Ta'iah Harden?" We jumped up and rushed over to see what news she had for us.

"That's us. What is going on, doc?"

"Well, Ms. Harden suffered a concussion and a broken leg which we repaired in several places. She appeared dehydrated, and her blood pressure was extremely low, which was the cause of her passing out, and that nasty fall down the steps. We are running I.V. fluids and keeping her sedated since she had slight swelling on her brain. But all in all, she and baby are good, thank God."

"Wait a minute. Did you say baby?" Justice asked the doctor.

"Yes, Ms. Harden is around seven weeks pregnant. We will be keeping her for a few days to monitor her and the baby's progress. Ms. Harden will be under heavy sedation for the next twenty-four to seventy-two hours to be certain her body is healing properly. We will gradually take her down once we are sure the swelling on her brain is under control. Do you have any questions?"

"Yes, who do we need to speak with to have her moved to a private suite? Her husband and mine are very high-profile men, and we don't need the media making a circus of this. We just want her healing to be as easy as possible," I told the doctor.

"Why, of course. We will have the accommodations arranged. In the meantime, I will allow you to visit Ms. Harden while she is in recovery, waiting for transport."

It only took them about five minutes to come and get us. When we entered Ta'iah's recovery room, it damn near broke my heart to see her hooked up to so many machines. She was intubated, and I saw where her leg was in a cast and elevated. Her vitals were displayed on the monitor, and the monitor connected to her stomach allowed us to hear the baby's heartbeat. I leaned over and kissed her forehead.

"Sis, you gotta get better. You have so much to live for, and we will be by your side all the way."

They came to transport Ta'iah to her private quarters, and we followed them upstairs. There was a pull-out couch in the room, and that was where I intended to stay. I told my husband to go to the store to get me a few outfits and toiletries. I would not be leaving her side until she woke up, and we could figure out what the next steps for our family were.

Justice came back with everything I asked for plus more. He managed to stop and get me a blanket, pillows, and slippers from the store. I kissed my wonderful husband goodnight and then prepared to lay it down. I just knew that when she woke up, we were going to have so much to discuss.

Chapter 21: Ta'iah

I had been having the most beautiful dreams ever. In these dreams, Dominant chose to reconsider breaking our arrangement. He finally came back home, and we were happy and content. In my dream world, he was back to being my everything. Dominant had me tied up and was about to spank me, and my core was dripping in excitement at the first lash. Then out of nowhere, this shrill beeping was causing Dominant to fade to black. The louder the noise got, the further away Dominant went. *Noooooo, I just got him back!*

My eyes popped open, and my surroundings were unfamiliar. It appeared that I was in the hospital, but how did I get there? The last thing I remembered was getting ready to go and beg Dominant's forgiveness and ask him to come back home. Then as I was on my way to complete my mission, everything went black.

Alarms started blaring, and people began rushing into the room. In all of the excitement, I saw Pure right on their heels. Almost immediately, they started poking and prodding me, taking my vitals, and gauging my cognizance.

"Hello, Ms. Harden, you gave your family quite a scare. We are about to remove the tube in your throat, and it will feel uncomfortable, so try not to panic." My eyes grew wide. Pure rushed to my side and grabbed my hand in a comforting manner. That helped my nerves calm slightly but not by much.

They prepared to take the tube out, and uncomfortable did not adequately describe the feeling. It felt like my throat was on fire. The doctor made it fast, and I was grateful for that small mercy.

"Now, one of the nurses will give you some water. I know your throat is feeling sore, but take small sips instead of big gulps. It will make drinking it easier."

I did as she said. It was hard because my mouth felt desert dry, and my dehydration made me want to swallow it fast. That water was everything on my tongue, and I was starting to feel refreshed, but honestly, I just needed someone to tell me how I got here.

"What happened?" That's all I could get out because my throat felt like I was swallowing glass.

"When we came over to check on you, we found you unconscious at the bottom of the staircase," Pure explained to me, and I guessed that made sense. I did remember feeling light-headed before everything went black. I just didn't remember much after that.

"Yes, young lady, and thank heavens, they found you when they did. You came into the emergency room severely dehydrated with your blood pressure dangerously low. There was slight swelling on your brain due to your spill down the stairs. Your tibia shattered in three places, but we were able to repair your leg. You will have to keep a cast on for six weeks and then have a few sessions of physical therapy. All in all, you and babies are doing well." The doctor explained my diagnosis plainly.

Wait. What. Did the doctor just say, babies? As in more than one. It was then that I noticed another machine in the room with separate vital signs than my own. I burst into tears. Dominant said he would own my womb, and he had done that literally. He left me flowers in my garden to grow.

Pure leaned over and gathered me in her arms, and it was surprisingly comforting. I had never been an overly emotional nor touchy-feely person, but this felt like the love of family.

"Pooh, why are you crying? A baby is a good thing," Pure told me.

"No, I'm not upset. I'm thrilled. It's just I didn't even know I had a little love muffin, or should I say muffins, inside of me. If I had known, I would have been doing my best to care for myself. Doctor, are you sure everything is okay with my babies?"

"Most certainly, all of the tests came back normal for a woman who, by my estimation, turned twelve weeks pregnant today."

The feeling I experienced at the news was surreal. I was going to be a mother. Who would have thought that a precarious situation would lead to something more significant than both of us? I wondered if Dominant had heard the news.

"Where is Dominant? Is he on his way here?"

Pure gave me a look and subtly shook her head in the negative. That just about became my undoing.

"Doc, can you give my sister and me a moment in private?" Pure asked the doctor.

"Of course. I will have somebody bring her lunch up, and if she can hold down her next three meals, we may be able to discuss discharging her late tomorrow or the next day."

The doctor left us alone, and Pure came to sit next to me. She held my hands, and to me, she may as well have been invisible because I was distraught. How could he not be here? Maybe I misjudged him and the caring role he played. It was my fault because he told me not to fall in love. Like an insolent child, I did the opposite and fell hard anyway. I was confident that I read our vibe correctly, but clearly, I was sadly mistaken.

"Sis, tell me what's wrong?" I didn't even know how to articulate to Pure the devastation that pierced my soul.

"I just don't know where to begin."

"Would your dilemma have anything to do with the items I found in your purse?" I turned red with embarrassment at Pure's question.

"Oh my God! I'm so embarrassed. I didn't mean for anybody to see that."

"Girl, boo, we as couples tend to get a little kinky. I am a free spirit when it comes to sex. However my man wants it, he can have it. I was interested in some things I saw inside that jumbo bag of tricks."

"Pure, it goes a little deeper than that I'm afraid."

I started to tell her everything about the dynamics of Dominant's and my relationship. Explaining to her the ins and out of our dom/sub lifestyle. I didn't know why, but she made me feel comfortable enough to share. She clutched her pearls at a few things, and she inquired about other things. At no point in time did I feel like she was judging me.

"Oh, my word, never have I ever. You two are like the *Fifty Shades of Grey* from the hood."

"For lack of a better analogy, yes. The thing is I fell in love with your brother-in-law, and he asked me not to do that. Now I don't know how he will take this news."

"I know my bro, and he will not shirk his responsibilities. I think you underestimate what he feels, because the dynamics of your relationship are a little unconventional. He is going through some deep things, and once he clears that up, I'm certain that your pregnancy will make him happy."

I wanted to believe everything that she said to me. With how things ended between us, I was a little doubtful. But then I had a bright idea. I wanted to be Dominant's greatest blessing. Something Pure said made me pause, and I knew exactly what to do.

"Pure, I need your help with something. I don't want any of you to mention this or the baby to Dominant. Once he figures himself and his issues out, I want him to come home to something he never expected."

After making our plans, she informed me that her husband and Papa were going to visit Dominant for a family intervention. I'd made Pure promise not to say anything to Dominant other than they checked on me, and I was okay. If it all worked out, I would give him something to change his perception of everything.

For the last four weeks, I had been at my cabin in the Poconos. I had no access to the outside world. Nothing but me, myself, and my thoughts. I'd been fishing, walked in nature, and just enjoyed the quiet. Any other person would probably have gone insane, but not me. The silence was soothing to my soul and healing my mind.

For years, I had led a busy life to drown out the issues I faced since my youth. Truly out of sight, out of mind. I just didn't have it in me to live through it and then dwell on it, but the choice had been taken from me.

I sat outside in a rocking chair, just listening to the birds sing. It was such a beautiful sound coming from a fantastic creature. I sat pondering on how the life of the bird is one to admire. The birds leave out every day and don't know where their meals are coming from until God led them to their meal. How I wish I could be as trusting and reliant as these beautiful creatures.

I heard a car approaching. I stood and shaded the sun rays out of my eyes. The truck pulled up and stopped right in front of the door. When its occupants got out, I broke out into a huge smile and hurried down to greet them.

"Twin, Papa, what are you guys doing here?" We were hugging and clapping backs for a few minutes.

"Son, you knew we would never let you face things alone. I missed you, so an old man had to come to lay his 20/20's on you." My Papa was why I loved my family. When faced with a trial, they didn't let you fold. They come and support you. It was a marvelous feeling to see my brother and grandfather.

"Dom, you been out here trying to become a lumberjack?" Justice had jokes because I had on a traditional plaid shirt with some jeans and hiking boots. It got cold as hell up here in the mountains.

"Very funny, nigga. Y'all come on inside and let's catch up."

The Cabin in itself was luxurious but didn't have modern amenities like T.V. or game systems. I do have Wi-Fi, but I had not plugged into the outside world and for a good reason.

"If you are here, then where is my sister-in-law?" I asked Justice because those two were joined at the hip

"She is headed back to Atlanta to deal with things with the company. Also, she is going to get the in-law suite together for Papa since he will be moving down there with us." All very good, but I was trying to work up the nerve to ask about my kitten.

"And Ta'iah, is she well?" I had to know to alleviate my fears.

"She is good. Pure talked her into coming out to the A for some girl time. You know how convincing Pure can be. Ta'iah didn't stand a chance against her charms."

We shared a laugh because Pure was convincing. I visibly relaxed because if she was around my family, at least she would have some support to deal with my absence. Although I chose to end our contract, it didn't mean that I wasn't concerned about her wellbeing.

I cared for Ta'iah in my own unique way. I just wasn't used to expressing my emotions. Oh, how I wished things between us could have been different, but that wasn't important at the moment. I needed to get to the bottom of my family disrupting my time of peace.

"Well, I'm happy to see you guys, but what bought you guys out here to the boondocks?"

A look between them, so I knew it's going to be something I wouldn't like, so I just prepared myself for the bullshit.

"Well, son, with everything that has happened, I thought it would be nice to have your family around to work through your pain. I feel responsible, and I won't leave you until you are healed."

I couldn't get mad at that. I was finally in a place where I thought I could open up to my family. They had already witnessed the worst of it, so a few more stories wouldn't kill me.

"Papa, I'm fine. I don't blame you at all. You honestly did everything you were supposed to do for your family."

While my family and I sat around talking, there was a knock at the door. I wasn't expecting anybody, so I looked at my brother. He had a suspicious look on his face, and I knew that he or whatever was on the other side of that door was set to piss me off.

"So, let me go get the door," Justice said before rushing out of the room.

When he came back in, he wasn't alone. There is a lady with him. She stood five feet tall with brown eyes and locs that were braided in an intricate design leading up into a bun. Her attire consisted of a white tunic and long, white, flowy skirt. Her face held no makeup, but her skin was radiant, making it hard to guess her age.

"Justice, what do you have going on?" My voice was elevated and the only warning Justice had before I started going berserk.

"Listen to me, bruh. Before you even fly off the deep end, I want you to understand that we have your best interest at heart. I agreed with Papa's idea just to come here and bond with you, but I feel that we truly need help as a whole for this to get healed properly. So, I researched a professional that could help guide this process."

"So, you brought a shrink?" I asked incredulously. Now I was supposed to be vulnerable in front of a woman I didn't even know.

"Little boy, I am not a shrink. I am a family therapist, and I have been in practice longer than you have been alive. My job is just to guide you to the answers you could already have but may not be able to see. Now apply your ass to a seat, and let's get to it. I don't have but a few good years left, and you won't waste my time," she scolded and then exited stage left, and very regally might I add.

She went to take a seat, and I saw my Papa looking at her in wonderment, and that made me smile. So, like a scolded child, I took my ass and sat with my arms folded and waited for the session to begin.

"Now, Holloway family, thank you for inviting me. My name is Dr. Carter, and I am here to help your family not only face your issues but to build a strong structure of support. What people fail to realize is that a family is like a body. Everybody has a functioning part for the body to work. I will help everyone find their places so that we can encourage your body to heal.

"This healing has to be something you are ready to undertake. I will dig deep, and it won't always feel good, but if you do the work, you will come out of this feeling renewed. Are we understood?" We all nodded in the affirmative.

"Now, let's start with the leader of your family. Mr. Holloway—"

"Blessed is fine." My papa cut her off so that she could call him by his first name. If I wasn't mistaken, his voice got all Billy Dee deep and made her blush. Aww man, Papa was trying to put his mac game down.

"Blessed, that is an excellent name. I understand from what you and Justice have shared with me that you guys found out your wife was molesting Dominant as well as his father. Tell me how finding out your wife had an illicit relationship with not only your son, but your grandchild as well, has affected you." That was news to me, so I listened attentively.

"I feel broken. A man does not build a family for it to be torn down from within. I feel like I invited a monster into my family. Not only invited her, but elevated her to a position where she felt untouchable enough to get away with this."

"That feeling is understandable. Were there any clues that something this devastating was taking place under your roof."

"Not at all. I worked a lot. I was a railroad technician for Amtrak, so I worked long hours and doubles at a minimum of one day a week…"

"Thursdays," I said, remembering his schedule as it was pivotal in the issue.

"Yes, Thursdays for the most part because I wanted to be available on the weekends to do extracurricular activities with you and your brother," my Papa clarified.

"Okay, Dominant, you interjected Thursdays into the conversation. Is that day important to you?" she asked me, and I began sweating profusely.

"Yes, I remember that Papa used to do doubles on Thursdays. Three to eleven, and then eleven to seven. I hated Thursdays and still do." I didn't think I could do this.

"Dominant, you're doing well. Tell your family why you hate Thursdays." I felt like I was hyperventilating, but I knew I had to get it out.

"Thursdays was the day she chose to come into my room and violate me. Every Thursday without fail, she'd do the sickest things to me. Shit, I can't do this. I gotta get out of here." I stood up to leave, but her words stopped me in my tracks.

"Running won't change what happened. Yes, she abused you, but that is not bigger than you confronting the hurt. Until you face the demons head-on, you will always be plagued with what happened, and guess what? She wins."

That took the flight right out of me. I knew I had to

tell my story, or it would never be over. I couldn't allow

her to continue to win. It was time to unburden my heart.

Chapter 23: Blessed

Watching my grandson go through so much anguish served to further break me down. The guilt I held in my heart was all-consuming. Dominant retook his seat, but he still looked frazzled. Dr. Carter allowed him to catch his breath and get his emotions under control.

"I'm glad you decided to stay. I can only imagine how it feels to relive these moments, but I promise you that once you let it out, you can leave it here, and we can find a way to move on from it." Her voice was mesmerizing and comforting like honey on sore vocal cords.

"Dominant, tell me if you can remember when her abuse started. Be sure to describe your feelings, so you are working through them," Dr. Carter instructed Dominant.

He peered at me, and I could tell that he was scared to damage my heart further. I nodded my head in reassurance, letting him know that it was alright. Dominant turned to her and began speaking.

"It started about two weeks after our parents died, and we moved into our grandparent's home. That night I thought I had a wet dream, but it was Nan giving me oral as I slept. When I saw it was Nan, I automatically tried to stop her. I knew what she was doing was not right, and I implored her to stop. She just laughed at me.

She began telling me how I enticed and teased her with having myself on display. I didn't understand how going shirtless was me inviting her to my body. It was as if she saw nothing wrong in having sexual thoughts about me. Even with all she revealed, I still begged her not to do it so that we could forget it happened. Her response was to threaten me with the one thing that mattered most. She told me if I didn't give in that she would do what she was attempting to do with me to my brother. I couldn't allow her to do that, so I let her live out her sick fantasies on me instead." My tears poured down my face in empathy at his pain.

"Had you ever been intimate with the opposite sex before that day?" Dr. Carter asked him.

"No, that night was the first time. She took my virginity amongst other things that night."

"What other things did she take that night?"

"She took my pride and freedom. That night, she vowed to break me and ruin me for any woman after her. In a sense, she did because she introduced me to a new world I never knew existed."

"Care to elaborate on that."

"My nan didn't want to just take my body. She was determined to dominate me. Own my mind. She molded me into a perfect slave. Anything she wanted, she commanded it, and it happened. My body was so in tune with her abuse that although I was repulsed and disgusted, my body afterward, unwillingly took part in the pleasure she offered."

"Okay, so she made you her sub. That doesn't seem like a role you play well. How was she able to make you submit?" I think they lost me with all of the rhetoric they passed back and forth regarding roles and submitting.

"Knowing that she would try to break my brother. It wasn't easy to force myself, and many times she would beat me into submission. The thought that my brother could be a victim made me learn to pretend. I allowed her to take advantage of me with the things her sick mind told her to do. I knew it wouldn't be forever. I just had to fake it until I made it." That made me cry so hard because no child should have to go through that.

"Okay, let's backtrack to something you said. You said your Nan told you she would ruin you for all women that came after her. How are your relationships with women you date?"

"I don't date, and I don't do relationships."

"Care to explain that?" I was listening to them attentively now because I was curious as well.

"I have never been in what you would consider a traditional relationship. Dating is a foreign concept and not how I operate."

"Okay so in what capacity do you deal with women, if that is your preference, on an intimate level?" I hoped she was not questioning my grandson's manhood.

"I think you lightweight tried to ask if I was gay. I'm very much so straight. I deal with women in a capacity that works for me. Any woman I deal with knows coming into the arrangement, that it's about a mutually beneficial pleasure that I guide."

"Hmmm, interesting. So you are in situations that mirror the abuse you suffered—whips, chains, and handcuffs." What type of freaky-deeky things was my grandson into?

"In a sense, yes and no. I pretty much operate in the dom/sub capacity in my situations, but it's more than sex. Having control over an individual just does something for me; it's euphoric. To have someone that is pliant and willing to be molded is soothing and works best for how I govern my life. It's as close to intimacy as I'm willing to get. My need to control every facet of my life makes me perfect for this role."

"Son, do you be doing the things the white folks write about? You are letting women tie you up and step on your balls, wearing them body condoms. Son, tell me you not somebody pet." Everybody just laughed, but I was oh so serious.

"No, Papa. I am what you would call a dominant or dom. Any woman I enter into an agreement with would be my submissive or sub. That means she accepts bending to my will. It can get kinky and involve them being tied up or spanked. Still, for me, it's more than just raunchy sex. It's about anticipating my needs and meeting them with a willing attitude. A woman that submits as natural as breathing." Oh, my child was all types of messed up inside

"What you're saying is that through dominating women, it helps you keep the control you felt was taken from you," Dr. Carter assessed, and she was on point.

"I never thought about it like that, but yes. I'm most comfortable in the role of a leader, especially when it comes to how I relate to a woman. I have to keep my feelings separate."

"Has there ever been a time when a dom/sub relationship has crossed into something of a normal relationship? If so, how did you deal with that?" Dr. Carter asked him, and Dominant thought for a minute before he answered.

"Yes, and if a woman decides she wants to turn this into a loving relationship, I will break the contract. That is why most times, I don't have sex with my subs, because lines get blurred."

"You mean to tell me that in over a decade of you living this lifestyle, your heart has never leaned towards a woman? Not one woman had you wanting to change the dynamics of your relationship?" Dr. Carter was digging deep with the questioning because my boy looked uncomfortable. Still, sometimes you had to get uncomfortable to get it together.

"Well, there has been one woman," Dominant told her as shyly as a young boy discovering his crush for the first time.

"Okay, tell me about her." My grandson's eyes lit up with excitement, and his thoughts came spilling out.

"She was perfection personified. There is not a need that I have that she doesn't meet. I push the limits with her sexually, and she never folds. She was the best thing about waking up in the morning and the peace I needed at night.

She knew my moods and how to appease them." My boy had a goofy look on his face that was all too familiar.

"How does she make you feel outside of the sex and control you need in your relationship?" He seemed to be thinking

"Her smile lights up my day. She laughs at my corny jokes. She is the first woman I laid next to, outside of sex, and it didn't repulse me. When she is around, I feel grounded. I found myself wanting to know her on a deeper level but didn't know how to get past what happened to me or changing our arrangement without appearing weak."

"She sounds amazing, so what happened to her?"

"Well, she was there the night that my secrets were revealed. Knowing that she witnessed such a weak moment made me feel unworthy of leading her. For the first time in my life, I was vulnerable in front of the opposite sex, and it unnerved me. So, I broke our contract and left. I couldn't deal with her watching me be weak. It did something to my pride. It made me feel out of control, and I don't know how to function unless I'm in control."

"Thank you for sharing these pieces of yourself with us. I know how society makes our men feel that they have to be strong. Placing the world on your shoulders and expecting you to hold it up without complaint. What has happened to you is not that uncommon in black families. You hear the whispers, but we don't take the time to address these issues head-on.

"We are taught that what happens in a family stays in a family. We don't create safe spaces for our children, especially the boys, to let us know when something is wrong. We teach them from an early age, not to cry when they hurt. Not to show emotion when something is bothering them. And to just take whatever comes your way because you are boys.

"I am here to tell you that being a man is not measured by how much you internalize, but how you can address adversity. It does not take away from your strength to feel it fortifies those feelings." Wow, she just gave an old fool a lesson real quick, and she wasn't finished schooling us.

"Let me leave you with this food for thought. You use your control as a security blanket because, in essence. You are afraid to be hurt and make yourself vulnerable. Maybe it wasn't that you felt unworthy to lead her but that for the first time, you felt worthy of being loved, and you didn't know how to let her. Now, one of you dashing gentlemen lead me to my sleeping quarters. These old bones are tired." I jumped right up to lead her out like the gentleman I was raised to be.

"Here, sugar, let me." I was on the prowl using my best charm in the presence of a queen.

"Oh, no you don't, you sly fox. I have been around long enough to know when somebody is making googly eyes at me. Won't be trying to get any of this fine wine without courting me properly. No, sir, I am from the old school. You are going to work hard to win me.

"But know that I feel your energy, and after we are done healing your family, I will let you feel mine too." She kissed my cheek and had me blushing like a young boy. Justice escorted her to her room, and we all retired to our separate dwellings. I think the doc was just what this family needed to pull it together. Time would surely tell.

Chapter 24: Ta'iah

It has been about four months since my fall down the steps and finding out that I would be a mother. After leaving the hospital and coming back to the house, I packed up and went to stay in Atlanta with Pure, where she nursed me back to health as well as became more than a friend. She had been so valuable to me and my not losing myself to my thoughts.

It was also in Atlanta that I found out that I would have twin girls, and I didn't know why, but it gave me a new lease on life. It was like finding out I was having daughters made me feel closer to their father. When I found out we would have two little girls I was over the moon with excitement, so I named our princesses Dahmia and Dahiah. I hoped he agreed with the names, because I used them whenever I talked to them, and they felt perfect.

I stayed in Georgia for two months and then decided to go back home. I realized that I was a business owner, and my absence was hindering my career. When I got back home to Philadelphia, I threw myself into my work. I had been working more from home and utilizing the shop Dominant had built for me in his home. We had a few new products coming out, and I needed to contact Anita and see how sales were going in-store. I grabbed my phone and called her.

"Hello, best friend, what warrants this call?" Anita asked sarcastically, and it made me begin to cry.

"Sheesh, I can't just miss my best friend? Have I been that bad to you?"

"Aww, babes, no, I was just teasing. Stop crying, crazy woman, and tell me how you and my beautiful nieces are doing." I sucked up my tears fast at the mention of my love muffins. My daughters were my favorite subject to talk about, and it always made me happy to talk about them.

"They are fine. I can't wait to see their faces. I feel about as big as a house. I'm eating everything and not getting any exercise. I can't see my feet or ankles." Anita giggled at my theatrics.

"You make it seem so hard. You are eating for three, so I'm sure your appetite has increased. Your journey to motherhood is a beautiful one. Just know that whatever you are facing is all to bring those new lives into the world. You are very fortunate." I heard the sadness in her voice, and it was my turn to be there for my friend.

"Pooh, are you okay? Still no word on Sterling?"

"No, and I don't know why he can't face me. I forgive him, and I just want him to forgive himself. I don't blame him at all. I just hope he doesn't blame me for what I have done. He is so reclusive he could be anywhere."

"What did you do that would make him leave?" I asked her curiously

"I did nothing to make him leave, but I doubt he will be coming back." Well, okay, I would just leave that conversation where it was if she didn't want to talk. She knew where to come if she needed an ear.

"Well, don't give up. You know I'm right where you are. I feel everything you're going through, but if you think that Sterling is worth it, wait for him."

"I hear you. I know it's not common to cross these emotional lines. I will cut my emotions off just to have Sterling direct me again." I got where she was coming from. I didn't need anything but Dominant's leadership. Everything else, children included, was a bonus. We finally shook off our sad thoughts and discussed business.

Anita told me sales and traffic to our store had increased since we unleashed our new line of vibrators with anal & clitoral stimulation added. I was happy to hear that, because I worked hard on that outside of the box idea.

We finally hung up after setting a date for lunch and saying our I love yous. I got up from my workbench and stretched my limbs. These babies were so active, and sitting for long periods made my joints lock up. While I was in my musings, my phone pinged with a text message

My Sissy Pure: Hey, love muffin, just wanted to let you know everything is a go for tomorrow. Are you excited????

Me: Yes, you just don't even know. I just hope it all comes together

My Sissy Pure: Girl bye! You know that all your hard work is going to pay off. I can't wait to see his face.

Me: You don't think he will be upset to find out like this? Were you able to get the team for the setup and break down?

My Sissy Pure: Get off my phone. You know everything is going to be suitable for your perfect patty having ass. Now you go and put those feet up. The glam

team from Pressed Hair Studio and I will be there to get

you together. Yolanda has some words for you chile.

Me: Tell her crazy self don't come here starting

with me. I overslept and missed my last appointment she

knows I got two people in my belly

My Sissy Pure: I got you boo. Love you to pieces

Me: Love you more

I was ready to go put my feet up and relax before

the team got here. That Yolanda and Saleema were crazy

but did the hell out of some hair. I had to be prepared for all

types of shenanigans with them fools.

Tomorrow was my baby shower and also a

welcome home celebration. That thought alone had me

giddy with excitement. Tomorrow would be life changing. I

just hoped it was in a good way.

Chapter 25: Dominant

Four months later, and I felt like a new man. I was so glad that my family decided to come and stay with me. I didn't know how Justice managed to get my sister-in -law to let him stay the whole time, but I was grateful.

Dr. Carter had been a godsend. She forced me to face some of my darkest demons. I never thought I could cope with having my innocence taken nor have a way to remove my nan from the space she rented in my head, but here today, my mind was free. I knew that things didn't happen overnight, but I was still doing the work.

Today was Thursday, and I didn't hate it as much as I used to, but it was still a point of contention for me, but I wasn't angry today. I could breathe easily and that more than anything else made a man feel good.

"You ready, bro?" Justice asked me.

"Sure, let me just grab my blazer. Where are we going again?" My brother came in with a garment bag.

When I looked inside, I saw this dope ass blazer done in royal purple and gold kente cloth pattern. Justice paired it with a white tee, white linen slacks, and some purple loafers. This outfit was on that grown man shit. Justice said we had an important company event, but he couldn't remember who was giving the event.

"Oh, it's just some artist showcase or whatever," Justice replied nonchalantly.

"Well, why do I have to go?"

"I haven't seen my wife in four months, so when she told me to bring you, I knew it wasn't up for debate. So you will show up, smile, and enjoy it. I'm trying to get my dick wet tonight." I burst out laughing because he was dead serious.

"Okay, bro, I got you. I will do anything for sis. You know that."

I turned to my twin, and he matched my fly but with his own twist. Justice had on linen shirt and slacks, but instead of a blazer, he had a bow tie and handkerchief in the same pattern as my blazer. This fool even got the fabric placed on his loafers. He just had to be extra, but I loved him anyway.

We checked out of the hotel we'd stayed in last night. We dropped Papa off the previous night because he said he had something to do. I think he was taking Dr. Carter on a date. If so, that would be good for him. He deserved to be happy.

The reason I chose to stay in a hotel was that I dreaded going home to an empty house. Also, I wanted to be alone with my twin. I had to make sure that he was good with everything that came out in our sessions.

I noticed that he blamed himself for my choosing to take the abuse in his steed. I'd let him know that I would take that and more just to ensure that he never knew pain. He broke down crying in front of me, and for the first time in a long time, I didn't clown him. I joined Justice in that much-needed cry and released the last of the pain. After the tears dried, the weight of the pain had been lifted, and I felt renewed.

We were in the car, and the venue was a good thirty-five minutes away from the hotel. I buckled in to enjoy the ride with my favorite guy. We were driving for about five minutes or so when Justice broke the silence.

"So, bro, I got some questions."

"Okay, shoot," I told him

"Now I was looking into some of dem kinky things you were talking about with Dr. Carter. Do you think I can try some of those things out at home with Pure? I mean, I don't think I can do the be in control of her all day every day because she would probably shoot me, but some of those things look like fun." He spit that out like he couldn't wait to ask me that.

"Yeah, twin, it's all about the confidence you possess. I will help you set up a night, and you can blow her mind and get your mind blown. Ta'iah has a website for spicing up the bedroom."

Why did I even have to say her name? It had been the hardest thing for me to admit that I lost something so important. I felt a tremendous amount of shame for the way I left her. Often, I wondered how she was faring and if somebody else had her under their tutelage. Then I would become instantly pissed for even thinking of another man touching her.

I couldn't be mad because my kitten begged me to stay, and I left her in this world all alone. Continuously, I beat myself up about that decision. It was the one decision that I would regret to the end of my days. It was nothing that I could do about it now.

We pulled up to the venue, and I pulled the visor down to check my greatness once more. We hopped out of the car, looking like we owned the place. Before we could make it in the doors, Justice touched my arm, so I stopped to see what he needed.

"I just wanted to say that I love you, and just know that your past doesn't define you. You can have any future you want. You just need to choose it." Justice's statement almost made me tear up.

"Thanks, bro. Your support means a lot. I'm ready for some new things in life. Who's to say, I might even find me a Pure and have some babies and relax in the south like you."

"You might find that sooner than you think."

His words puzzled me, but I didn't even have time to ponder on that. We entered the hall, and it was decorated with grandeur. Coincidentally, the décor matched my blazer, and it struck me as odd. Justice was walking a little ahead of me as I took in my surroundings. When I got to the doors, it said *"Welcome to Royalty"* on the banner.

When I stepped through the doors, it was like stepping into a time warp machine. The décor was indicative of ancient Egypt all around. The hall sported everything Egyptian from cats to sphinx. The tables had canopic jars for centerpieces.

As I walked through the space, I saw some faces I knew and some that I didn't. When I looked closer, I saw a good mix of Asians and African Americans. It was a multi-cultural vibe, and I was looking forward to seeing some new talent.

I was making my way around the room, and for some reason, I gravitated to the middle. The center of the hall appeared to be where the main attraction was taking place. Right there, in the middle of the floor, was a larger than life Pyramid replica. Servers were dressed in traditional Egyptian garments while fanning the pyramid's inhabitants. When I moved closer, there stood another banner that said *"Kingdom Holloway Welcomes Princesses Dahmia and Dahiah."*

I was confused as hell because anytime Justice got my sister-in-law pregnant, he announced it to the world like he was the only man whose soldiers marched. I stepped into the pyramid, and Papa and Dr. Carter sat on throw pillows wearing what I now understood to be the theme of the event. Papa was looking real dapper in slacks, shirt, and suspenders with the matching bowtie that matched my blazer. Dr. Carter had on all white with a traditional African head wrap in the print of my blazer. I looked to the left, and Pure wore traditional African garb, including the head wrap in my blazer's print. Okay, so that was the fam, but who were we celebrating?

I stepped fully into the pyramid, and my feet stood upon gold silk and lilies. I followed the flower's trajectory, and it led me to a pair of throne seats. One of the throne seats was empty. The other place was occupied by none other than Ta'iah. My kitten sat, shoulders back, and head held high, showcasing all of the regal beauty she embodied. Her hair was twisted up into a bun with lily buds woven into it to make a crown. Ta'iah's garment was sleeveless and matched my blazer perfectly. Her feet were bare, but it was what she carried in the middle that had me stuck. I massaged my chest as my heart constricted in pain. She was beautiful, and after all these months of not seeing her, it all came rushing back.

Ta'iah was talking to a couple that you could tell held the recipe for the mixture that created her perfection. As soon as Ta'iah noticed me, her gaze lowered, and she dropped her head in a subtle nod of acknowledgment. Even with all of the time spent apart, she still acquiesced to my dominance.

"Ta'iah, come!" She snapped right to attention and stood to her beautiful feet, with some struggle, but she moved to me fast. When she reached me, her hands were to her sides, and her head was bowed. My eyes traveled her body head to toe in inspection once more. She was ripe and pregnant. I kneeled in front of her and just gazed at her belly in wonderment. There was no question that what Ta'iah carried inside of her womb belonged to me. I placed my hands on both sides of her stomach and peppered kisses all over the baby bump.

I stood, and when we were once again face-to-face, I tipped her head back. She had tears in her eyes as I placed kisses all over her face, then her lips and lastly her forehead. I gathered Ta'iah close to my heart and held on for dear life before whispering in her ear.

"I gave you my legacy, and you kept it in your womb. Even when I left you all alone, you didn't hate me, and what you carry in your womb is proof enough. I will forever be grateful for this gift. We will discuss it all when we get home. Thank you, Kitten. I am so proud of you at this moment. Now let's go entertain our guests."

She took my hand and led me to the empty throne. I went away alone, thinking that I would have to begin my life over alone. Only to come home to a family and realized that life could begin anew.

Chapter 26: Ta'iah

I couldn't believe he was here, and not only here but happy. Initially, I didn't know how he would react to walking in and seeing my family and his gathered together. All of them there to celebrate the lives he didn't know existed. I expected him to come out of a bag on me, but he didn't, and I was grateful. Dominant took the news all in stride, and that was fortunate because the surprises didn't end there.

Dominant attended to my needs throughout our whole baby shower. He sat and rubbed my feet the entire time we opened gifts. Dominant made me eat until I was stuffed beyond belief. It was like he was making up for the lost time. He was laughing and joking, and it was good to see him in such an honest light.

We got everything we could have ever needed for a baby. We had everything from double strollers to diaper genies and gift cards to almost twenty thousand dollars in cash. The cash we would put into their college funds, and it was a blessing to have a village such as ours. As the night progressed, I started feeling tired. Noticing this, Dominant announced to our guest that we would be leaving early. Justice and Pure promised to pack our gifts up and bring them to the house in the next day or so.

Dominant helped me slip into my purple ballet flats. Then he hefted me up and took my hand to lead me out of the hall. Dominant held me so close to him, and I was enjoying his energy. He helped me up into the truck, and we made our way home.

As we drove home, we listened to smooth jazz and held hands, allowing the tunes to embrace our reverent silence. The closer we got to home, my thoughts ran rampant. I hoped my next surprise took the cake and went a long way to showing Dominant what he meant to me. When we got outside of the house, my emotions began to overwhelm me. We had not been together in this place in what felt like ages. Dominant parked the truck and came around to my side to help me down.

"What's the matter, Kitten?"

"Nothing, I'm fine, just a bit tired." I hated to tell the little white lie, but I wanted to build the suspense.

"Well, come on so I can draw you a bath and rub you down. Then it's straight to bed for you."

We entered the elevator headed up to our floor. Slowly, we were ascending, and tonight the journey felt unusually long. The bell finally dinged our arrival, and when the doors opened, all you saw was candles, silk lilies and rose petals along the walkway.

Down the walkway laid a purple and gold carpet, for verily a king had returned home. Dominant stood on the carpet, taking in the heavenly scene that greeted him. I slipped my shoes off before bending down to slip his off. I had forgotten none of my manners.

When I stood up, I took his hand and began walking him into the living room. Inside the living room, there was a projector playing. I also had a bed and a bench with a few of our favorite toys set up. Tonight, I intended to remind him of home, while at the same time, starting a new life built on our old one.

"Oh, Ta'iah, my perfect little kitten, you did this all for me?"

I just nodded my head. Dominant's eyes became transfixed on the screen hanging from the ceiling. I had a video of me at every stage of my pregnancy, from finding out what we were having to bestowing names upon the girls. There were even snippets of me reading to them and little love notes I'd written to him.

Dominant was crying freely, and witnessing his emotions sparked my emotions. Although I didn't tell him about the babies, as he was on his journey to healing, I didn't want him to miss anything. I headed over to the dresser and pulled out a piece of paper. On it, I had a new contract drawn up. This would be the moment of truth.

"Kitten, it's so perfect. Thank you for showing me this. I feel like I was there. I'm sorry you had to go through this alone."

"Daddy, it was not a lonely journey. My hope for your return kept me going. Knowing that you were away doing something necessary made it easy for me to endure for just a while. I missed you dearly, and at first, I didn't know how I was going to make it without your guidance. I needed you, but I needed you whole more."

I walked over to him and handed him the new contract and stepped back. With nervousness, I waited for him to accept or reject my terms. The silence was killing me. The ball was in his court.

Ta'iah handed me a piece of paper. I was a little perplexed, but I opened the note and began to read.

Life Contract

I Ta'iah Harden as submissive of Dominant Holloway promise to never:

- *Give my body to another individual other than Dominant Holloway*

- *Judge him for tender moments as they will only enhance the experience shared between Dom and Sub*

- *Stop being kinky and fulfilling every sexual need your appetite requires*

- *Stop loving you although you never knew it, but it is indeed true*

And I promise:

- *To continue to anticipate Dominant's every need to ensure that your happiness will always remain first*
- *To participate in all activities and duties described in the original contract*

All of these things I promise in addition to being a dedicated mother to your children, a friend when days get dark, to comfort you when you need peace, and become wife soon as you say yes to these terms. Daddy, please say yes!

I gazed up from the note, and Ta'iah appeared sick waiting for me to make a decision.

"I will say yes to these terms as long as you say yes to mine," I said to her.

"I will say yes to anything. Just tell me what I need to do." Ta'iah was always eager to please me, and that made my decision easy.

"I will say yes, as long as you allow me to love you in return."

She responded to my request by jumping in my arms. Her excitement made me do something I'd never done with a woman before. I grabbed her by the nape of her neck, and French kissed her beautiful full lips. I kissed her with all the passion inside of me as I savored her unique flavor, committing it to memory. I deepened the kiss, and if I could, I would've kissed her forever. No one told me a first kiss could be this mind-blowing.

Pulling my lips from hers, I just gazed at this beautiful woman. A woman who had hope in me when I didn't even have it for myself. One who gave herself to me freely without questions. Ta'iah was the most magnificent specimen ever created, and she was all mine. That thought alone had me ready to play. I stepped back and walked around her to sit on the bed.

"Did you miss daddy?"

"Yes," she responded immediately.

"Yes, what?" She automatically dropped her eyes to the floor. She caught on fast to the mood.

"Yes, daddy, I missed you very much."

"Kitten, come." She walked until she stood in front of me.

"Let me see how much you missed me. Lift your dress."

She grabbed the full skirt of her dress and lifted it until her bottom half was exposed. I touched her through her panties, and they were soaked through the fabric.

Pulling them to the side, I ran my fingers over her clit, and she started shivering.

"You better not cum yet. The games have just begun, Kitten."

I stroked her lazily. Then I dipped my fingers into her tight, gushy center and enjoyed the wetness that welcomed me back home. I removed my fingers and placed them in my mouth, licking them clean. That was another first for me. Ta'iah tasted sweet, and I want to give her a bunch of my firsts tonight. I was going to start with something that I'd been thinking about doing since we met.

"Remove your dress and panties and lay on the bed."

Ta'iah hurriedly disrobed before assuming the position. When she was on her back with her legs spread, I kneeled in front of the bed, and she automatically tried to sit up. She was not used to me being in a subservient

position, so I knew she was trying to figure out my end

game.

"Lie back down, Kitten. Do you doubt me?"

"I doubt you never."

"Good girl, enjoy what I am giving you. It's

something I've never willingly given a woman before. Tell

me what you feel, but the rules are still the same. You cum

when I tell you to. Do you understand?"

"Yes, daddy, I understand."

Once she was lying down once again, I removed my

blazer and my shirt. If my abuser taught me anything, it

was how to eat a mean box. I was about to change her life. I

pulled her to the edge of the bed, spread her knees, and

placed her feet flat. Her pussy was so pretty I almost didn't want to disrupt the picture by getting messy. But I was hungry, and with no hands, I dove in headfirst.

I licked all around her inner lips before placing a succulent kiss on her clit. From top to bottom, I devoured her pussy like the last meal of a death-row inmate. Ta'iah was shaking, shivering, and screaming as her juices poured out of her. She started stuttering and calling out to God

"Oh my God! Daddy, that feels so good. Permission to cum, please?" I sat up and wiped the remnants of the best meal of my life off my lips before responding.

"Permission denied."

I stood up and removed my pants because there was no way she would cum unless it was all over this dick. With my knees on the bed, I used my lower body to scoot her back. I crawled up her body while placing kisses in rare places all along the way. I was trying to show her what my words would never adequately convey.

Once I was positioned right between the softest place on earth, I leaned down to sip from her lips. Ta'iah kissed me back with such tenderness and adoration, my heart filled with joy. I picked her legs up and placed them around my waist. She was clenching and unclenching the sheets. It was then that I realized I'd never allowed her the pleasure of being intimate with me. I had never been intimate with any woman. It was the reason why I chose missionary. Tonight, I wanted Ta'iah to understand she inspired my changes. I'd hoped to convey that our relationship had elevated, and we weren't operating on old knowledge.

"You can touch me, Kitten."

Her eyes began to water, and it made me feel funny all in my chest. I leaned down and kissed her tears as they spilled down her cheeks. Then her hands became exploratory, sliding up my chest and around my back. Ta'iah was like a kid with a new toy, giddy with excitement. When she placed her hands around my neck and coaxed my head down for another kiss, I obliged her.

While we sipped from each other's lips, I slid home. A mutual gasp broke the silence of the moment. I almost lost my shit because her pussy was tighter, wetter, and warmer than usual. For a few moments, I stayed seated, trying to fight the overwhelming need to cum. My kitten became impatient as she started to gyrate her hips, pressing me to move. I slowed her urgency because this was my first time making love, and I wanted to enjoy the moment, so I began to give her slow deep strokes.

The feeling was so amazing. Ta'iah was so expressive and responsive to my ministrations. I was swimming in it and hitting her spot enough to make her tremble and lose her breath. As I tapped on that secret spot, Ta'iah began to look crazed.

"Fuck me, please! Daddy, I missed you! She missed you!" She asked so nicely, and I would deny her nothing.

Pulling out to the tip, I braced myself on my arms before slamming back inside. That was the pace I set as I began to beat her pussy out of the frame. I was hitting her so deeply and deathly that it had Ta'iah professing her love in two languages and screaming my name. The sound was music to my soul and had my heart catch a vibe. Suddenly, her walls clenched me, and it involuntarily made my nut rise to the top.

"Come with me *now!*" Ta'iah started squirting everywhere, and I dropped all of my seeds inside of her, and it felt like it would never stop.

I laid there for a moment and enjoyed the feeling of our re-connecting. By the time I caught my breath, I'd gone soft and could disengage our bodies. I rolled off of Ta'iah to lie beside her. Then I turned her on her side before bringing her flush against me and snuggling close.

"Ta'iah, thank you for welcoming me home."

"No, thank you for saying yes."

"Thank you for giving me a reason."

Just like that, I closed my eyes, and for the first time, I held a woman close and drifted off into a blissful sleep with no fears or apprehension about tomorrow.

Epilogue

Six months later

Today was a joyous occasion. Today we were holding a sip and see for our beautiful daughters, Dahmia and Dahiah. I was thrilled to show them off to the world. The night after I came home, I woke up to my usual morning ritual. It felt like I'd never left home. We ended up making love all morning long. It was in our third round that Ta'iah's water broke.

It was all a frenzy after her water broke. We made it to Jefferson, which ironically, she had been going there for prenatal care. We arrived, and once we got to the floor, she was checked into Labor and Delivery. When they checked her cervix, she had already dilated ten centimeters. Which she was happy about because she wanted to birth naturally.

Watching Ta'iah bring my legacies in the world was mind-blowing. She was calm as opposed to my freaking out. I held her hand and whispered sweet nothings in her ear. About thirty minutes after her arrival, she began pushing. The experience was almost religious to witness.

The moment I heard my princesses cry, my tears began to flow. It was humbling to know that my babies would depend on me to protect, teach, and love them into greatness. Right then, I vowed never to fail them or the womb that bore them.

"Hey, are you okay?" I turned to face the owner of this angelic voice and beamed with pride.

"Yeah, babe, I'm good. How are you feeling?" She rubbed her belly before returning my smile. We'd just found out Ta'iah was expecting again, and I was over the moon. This time around, I got to experience it from the beginning, and it had been amazing so far.

"I'm feeling okay. The girls are napping," she responded as she walked into my arms.

"You sure? I don't want you on your feet all day trying to please everyone else." I worried about Ta'iah and wanted her in tip-top shape while she housed my baby in her womb. She just rubbed her cheek against my chest affectionately at my overprotective behavior.

"I promise I have hardly done anything. Between Pure, Dr. Carter, and my mommy, I haven't had to do anything but give directions."

"That's a good girl."

We headed into the girls' room to get ready to take them down to meet the masses. They looked so adorable lying there like two little Nubian princesses. We used the same designer, J*Diza Clothing Co., who designed my blazer and her dress for the baby shower. Everything from the headbands to the little booties were perfect.

She hired the same event planner, Truly Bleu Events Unlimited, and I had to say she executed another perfect event. We had a royalty theme going on in our house. The little throne bassinets were set up on a raised dais to make it appear as if they were addressing the court.

In front of their little thrones, an area was set up so that the guests could lay gifts at their little feet. It was so beautiful and original.

I looked around and was delighted to see all of our family here to witness this moment. Being as though it was at our home, the guest list was exclusive. Privacy was something that I still valued and would protect at all costs. I turned around, and I saw Sterling coming toward me.

"Look at you, all domesticated and whatnot." I laughed heartily at this fool and pulled him into a manly embrace.

"Shut up, fool. How are you doing, man? I didn't think you were coming." He had been underground for the last year.

"I'm getting there. Thank you for referring me to Dr. Carter. You know I wouldn't miss the introduction to my nieces. I am their favorite uncle, you know."

"You and Zuri are killing me with the competition. Since he couldn't be here, I guess you are in the lead." We joked back and forth about who was the greatest uncle until our conversation was cut off by Ta'iah squealing.

"Nita, oh my God! When did you have the time? Why didn't you tell me you had a baby? We could have enjoyed the journey together. Oh my God, he is adorable. Let me see him. Hey, little man. I'm your auntie. Oh, I love him already. Dominant, come look."

My kitten never got overly excited, and that made us head in their direction. When we got to her, I saw Ta'iah's best friend and business partner Anita, standing there holding a baby. Sterling stopped, and all the color drained from his face. Then the mask dropped across his expression. He snapped his fingers once, and Anita's head snapped up, and when she saw him, her eyes fell. Sterling snapped twice, and Anita began walking over with the baby in her arms. When Anita arrived in front of Sterling, she stood with her gaze averted.

"Eyes up, love." She looked at him, and her gaze was watery.

"Show me." Anita hurriedly unwrapped the baby. One look into his honey-colored eyes and the matching birthmark on his cheek, and I could see that my friend had joined me in fatherhood.

"Love, please tell me that you didn't." Anita couldn't respond to him, as she was crying uncontrollably. Sterling took the baby from her and then did the unexpected and left out of the door. I didn't know what their story was or how it would end. We just had to wait and see.

Sterling and Anita's Story Coming Soon!

All businesses mentioned in this book are real, and

you can enjoy their products and services just like these

characters:

Knatural Kreations (Organic health and beauty

boutique)

FB:@knaturalkreationslive

IG:@knaturalkreations

Email: knaturalkreationslive@gmail.com

J*Diza Clothing Co, Brooklyn, NY 11208 347-815-

3492 jdizaclothingco@yahoo.com

www.jdizaclothingco.com

Truly Bleu Events Unlimited

Philadelphia, Pa 19124

267-522-BLEU(2538)

FB & IG:@trulybleuevents

Pressed Hair Studio

2040 Poplar Str.

Philla., Pa 19130

All About Nadine Frye

Nadine Frye was born and raised in Philadelphia, PA. But coming from the inner-city never stopped her ability to dream big. Being raised in a large family, we used our creative minds to have fun. Making plays and songs and any other things we could dream. In her younger years, you could see her head inside of a book more often than experiencing the outdoors.

In her teen years, a personal tragedy unleashed a world of sadness and hurt only her notebook could understand. Songs and poems poured from her soul, and for years, it was to feel the relief from her heart. She began sharing small things with her close circle of friends. It was their motivation and that of her mother and sisters that she shared her talent with the world. That was the beginning of dreaming bigger.

She now resides in Washington, DC, where she wears many hats, including Mother and Wife, and she graciously adds the hat of an author to her line up.

Personal Quote

"Life is about evolving. Each day is a journey, each year is a teacher, and every lesson should be applied." -Nadine Frye

Author Page:

https://www.facebook.com/PurpleLyricFandom/

Instagram: @authornadinefrye

Twitter: @AuthorNadine

Email: purplelyricfandom@gmail.com

Blog: https://authornadinereviewspor.blogspot.com/

CPSIA information can be obtained
at www.ICGtesting.com
Printed in the USA
LVHW041702061120
670968LV00006B/883

9 798649 231336